RUFFIAN ON THE STAIR

RUFFIAN ON THE STAIR

Nina Bawden

Thorndike Press
Waterville, Maine USA

This Large Print edition is published by Thorndike Press, USA.

Published in 2002 in the U.S. by arrangement with Curtis Brown UK.

U.S. Softcover ISBN 0–7862–3955–7 (General Series Edition)

The text of this Large Print edition is unabridged.
Other aspects of the book may vary from the original edition.

Set in 16 pt. New Times Roman.

Printed in Great Britain on acid-free paper.

Library of Congress Cataloging-in-Publication Data

Bawden, Nina, 1925–
    Ruffian on the stair / Nina Bawden.
        p. cm.
    ISBN 0–7862–3955–7 (lg. print : sc : alk. paper)
    1. Aged men—Fiction. 2. Parent and adult child—Fiction.
    3. Adult children of aging parents—Fiction. I. Title.
    PR6052.A84 R84 2002
    823'.914—dc21   2001054068

Madame Life's a piece in bloom
Death goes dogging everywhere
She's the tenant of the room
He's the ruffian on the stair.

W. E. HENLEY

ACKNOWLEDGEMENTS

To Dr Poulsen-Hansen (Freddie-next-door) who told me the saddest story. To Professor Elizabeth Simpson, who taught me all I am ever likely to know about transplantation antigen genes, to Bruce Page for lending me a wonderful book (which I must return sometime) about tools, and also to George, my father-in-law, who died at the age of 102 before he could express an opinion on the antics of my fictional centenarian.

The Mudd family, other branches of it, first appeared in *Familiar Passions*.

CHAPTER ONE

The last time you and I had dinner alone together was in that brothel in Baden-Baden.'

It is six days before Silas Mudd's hundredth birthday. Coral, his daughter-in-law, dining alone with him in his London club answers him loudly and patiently: 'No, Daddy, we went to the brothel but we didn't dine there.'

Daddy, she thinks. At her age. What a fool she is, always rushing into things. Twenty years ago, about to marry Will, she had said to his father, 'What shall I call you?' and he had said, unexpectedly and uncharacteristically diffident, 'What about Daddy? The children always called me Father. That was their mother, of course. She thought Father sounded better class.'

Although she had thought it absurd, Coral had been touched by this request and Silas's sudden, shy air and, anyway, she had wanted to please him: Will's ancient father, the lonely old widower, about to turn eighty. Had she known it would be for so long, she would have never agreed to it. But no one in her family had ever reached such an age, giving up the ghost, passing on, leaving earth or, in the case of the more forthright, just *dying*, in their early seventies if not in their sixties. How could she have guessed that within a few months 'Daddy'

1

would be rejuvenated, peacocking around in new suits, expensive ties, first courting then marrying his second wife, Bella?

She says, 'We had dinner in the hotel, Daddy. It was absolutely as dull as you said it would be.'

Will had been absent that evening, too. He and Coral had gone to Baden-Baden, partly to see Silas who was spending a month in a comfortable, if undistinguished, hotel that had offered him a special weekly rate, and partly so that Will could see one of his authors, a German who wrote in English because his Jewish parents had sent him to England to be educated before World War Two. Will thought this man's new novel might well be his last, a prospect that did not displease the international company that had recently taken over Will's small publishing house, keeping Will on as a consultant; although the novelist was still highly respected, his sales had declined as his age had increased. He also required, when it came to editing his manuscripts, rather more delicacy than some of the younger editors in the firm could willingly contemplate or thought worth the trouble.

Will had spent the afternoon with this difficult author and was to dine with him and his wife. Silas, gallantly keen to amuse his daughter-in-law, had suggested an expedition into the town. There was this restaurant he had noticed, shaded lights, discreetly romantic; he was sure she would like it. As she had entered, Silas on his two sticks following slowly, the bosomy Madame, rosy-fleshed, tightly corseted, rose out of the velvety gloom and murmured—Coral had thought for her ear alone, 'Would you like to leave your father and come back for him later?'

She had not thought Silas could have heard this: he was some way behind her, grappling with his sticks and the heavy curtain that shrouded the internal door, some sort of rubbery material, insulation from the continental cold, and he had been, even then, very deaf. Coral had told him the restaurant was closed, it was the end of the season, and he had limped after her back to the car and said nothing except what a pity: he was bored with the food in the hotel and had hoped for a little gastronomic excitement.

Of course, he had understood perfectly, she realises now. Kept it to himself all this time, just waiting for the chance to get her alone and come out with it.

She says, 'We had some kind of lake fish in thin grey sauce. And a greyish cream cakey thing afterwards. In appearance, much like the first course. Except for the bones.'

He nods. He remembers his meals. Measures his days by them. Well, she had remembered that one, hadn't she? And how long ago was it? After Dinkie was born.

3

Fourteen years, fifteen? The first winter Silas had been alone again.

Silas says, 'You stayed in that hotel with me several days. I expect we ate there on another occasion. But that night, I'm sure of it, you and I dined in the brothel.'

Coral hears—fancies she hears—a stifled giggle from somewhere behind her. Well, of course, Silas, being deaf, is given to shouting, and has to be shouted back to. He has an old hearing-aid that had belonged to Will's mother, hardly state-of-the-art any longer, but he refuses to update it; he isn't mean but he has better things to do with his money than waste it on pricey hearing devices. There have been other occasions in the club when Coral has felt their table was providing the floor show. A wary glance at neighbouring tables confirms that everyone in the dining room is sitting bolt upright, silent and listening. Like a lot of meerkats, she thinks, remembering a nature film on television. Long bodies, little heads, alert, quivering. Some kind of ground squirrel, or lemur. Somewhere in Africa? Or South America?

Silas has his back to the room. All the same he must know other guests would be able to hear them. Deaf, eyesight going, but mind and memory still well oiled, smoothly running. Is he enjoying this ridiculous public exchange? Having fun thinking he might be embarrassing her? Or, childishly—his *second* childhood—

4

paying her out for *not* leaving him in the brothel and coming back later? No, no, Silas would never do that. He is a steadfastly chivalrous old gent; still struggling to open doors, pull out chairs, all the old-fashioned courtesies.

She says, 'I didn't know you had realised what the place was. I suppose I was sparing your blushes. But really, Daddy, we didn't eat there. That wasn't quite the kind of service on offer.'

Coral speaks in her fullest voice, her famous reach-the-back-of-the-gods voice, not the sort of thing they teach at drama schools any longer. And Silas, in spite of the baffle of deafness, hears it clearly enough to understand what might have passed through her mind. Indeed, the faintest of colour tints his pale, waxy skin for perhaps thirty seconds.

He says, 'Club's pretty empty tonight, isn't it? Well, of course, Saturday. People away for the weekend.'

Coral forgives him. Perhaps he has been so busy pondering the delivery of his little jest about brothels in Baden-Baden, rehearsing it gleefully during his after-lunch nap, that he has really forgotten there would be other members dining this evening. Sitting with his back to them, out of his sight, they had slipped from his mind. Forgivable, *natural* indeed, in a man aged ninety-nine years, eleven months and three weeks. But he would hate to think

5

she might have thought that. She says, leaning forward, touching the plump blue veins on the back of his hand, 'Quite a few. As you well knew, you bad man.'

She shakes her head, laughing at him and with him, and he straightens his shoulders and lifts his chin, milky eyes sparkling. Preening himself. Coral, the actress, appreciates the effort he makes, putting on a good show for her. Not that she hasn't made an effort for *him*: she has dressed to please him this evening in her navy Jean Muir, several years old now but cut with the kind of elegant discretion she is sure he still admires. His wife, his *first* wife, mother of Will, Hannah and Alice, had been obsessional about her appearance, spending huge amounts in what, so Will had told Coral, she always referred to as 'little' dress shops (as if the use of the diminutive mitigated her extravagance) on well-cut suits and dresses in black, navy or grey that she cared for as if they were her delicate children, removing them immediately she returned from an outing, from a lunch or a shopping expedition, in case they should crease or get dirty, and hanging them to 'rest' in her closet.

*   *   *

It had been the one thing about Silas's second wife that had astonished Will and his sisters (not Coral, of course, who had never known

Mother) and, though none of them would admit it, slightly dismayed them. Bella wore bright, shiny clothes, always tightly belted and usually a size too small. 'The sort of things Mother would have called common,' Will had said to Coral, shrugging his shoulders and laughing a little to show that he didn't agree with this judgement even though he might comprehend it.

This apart, Silas's children had welcomed Bella even if, as far as his daughters were concerned, the main reason was their own convenience. Silas was a strong old man, but even strong old men grow dependent eventually, and when she married Silas, Bella was a healthy widow in her early sixties who had already buried two elderly husbands and could surely be relied upon to take care of a third until the ferryman called for him. Hannah and Alice, both only slightly younger than Bella, were particularly (if secretly and silently) conscious of the burden she had lifted from them. Will was too young to be expected to face up to the adult responsibility of an ageing parent. Or so his two older sisters, used to indulging their baby brother, considered. And yet, when the call came (from Athens, mid-February) it was Will who had answered it, abandoning Coral, about to give birth to their third child and already in hospital, to fly to his father's deathbed. The Greek doctors, Bella had said when she telephoned, thought

7

Silas might hang on another forty-eight hours but no longer. It was a quite *horrid* flu, she said, breaking off to cough herself, achingly. 'I blame myself,' she wailed. 'I went walking round the headland in the rain and I caught what I thought was *this cold*, and I gave it to him.'

On the drive to Heathrow, on the flight, Will had forced himself to put aside his concerns for Coral and the new baby and conscientiously examined his feelings for his father. Silas was eighty-six now, and though he would be sorry to see the old man go, so Will told himself, it was a good age, a fair innings, an outpouring of grief was hardly in order. 'No, no, not *in order* at all', he muttered, playing this over, this kind of gruff, so-called manly expression, and found himself on the edge of unsuitable laughter. He rang the bell for the stewardess, asked for a brandy, and when it came, gulped it down in an attempt to restore some kind of seemliness to his thoughts at this solemn moment. Did he love, had he ever loved, Father?

He dodged that one. He would miss him, of course. Why, Silas had been around *all his life.* That self-evident observation made Will snigger disgracefully; he blew his nose loudly and ordered another brandy. What he meant, he told himself sternly, was that while a man of his age had a father of Silas's age still alive, it kept the contemplation of his own death at bay.

Silas had always been an old man to Will, middle-aged and grey-haired when Will was born, Mother's late, menopausal baby from whose birth she had never recovered. Or so Will had been given to understand. Aged six or so, he had asked Silas, innocently, why (when she wasn't shopping or lunching or playing bridge) his mother was always lying down while other mothers were running about, playing ball games and swimming, and Silas had answered, 'You did that, boy, Mother gave life to you and very near lost her own, make sure you never forget it.'

Will had never repeated that remark to anyone, not even to Coral. As a little boy, he had been too ashamed: if people knew what he had done, they would hate him. How many knew, anyway? Fear made him shy with his parents' friends, who considered him sullen. Later, more or less grown, he thought no one would believe him, and if they did, might think he was asking for pity. Occasionally he had thought he might tell Coral as a sour sort of joke; if she laughed, he could put it behind him. But Coral was fond of Silas, and Coral's affection (Will was often uncomfortably aware of this) could be conditional. And he had *needed* her to be fond of Silas. His sisters lived so far away, one in the States, on a lake in Maine, the other only in Yorkshire but so immovable by habit as well as inclination that she might as well have lived in Australia. Not that Silas had been demanding. Within two months of Mother's death, he had sold the London house and taken entirely happily to living in clubs and hotels, never staying in one place longer than a few weeks, moving on as soon as the weather deteriorated or he was bored with the food. He liked to see Will when he was in London but when abroad a thrice-weekly telephone call, an occasional letter or fax, had been all he had appeared to expect. And once Bella had joined him in his agreeably nomadic existence he had been happy to leave all communication with his children to her. When they were coming to England it was Bella who made arrangements to see them, who sent postcards from various comfortable billets around the world, who chose Christmas and birthday presents. She had kept a house of her own in Nauplion, in the Peloponnese, a legacy from her second (Greek) husband, and this was the only 'home' Silas ever consented to stay in since he had got rid of his own. Bella had once said to Will, 'He isn't a domesticated man, is he? Do you think it might be why he has lived so long? Never had to wrestle with the boiler or change a lightbulb. I know he's *interested* in tools, but I've never seen him use one!'

Remembering this light-hearted speculation on the flight to Athens, Will wondered if it was true. He supposed that in her exhausted way,

10

Mother had run the family house while he was growing up, though what he actually remembered was a succession of kindly middle-aged ladies cooking, cleaning, and presumably changing the lightbulbs and wrestling with the boiler. He realised now that he had never seen his father in a kitchen. It occurred to him that it might have been staying in Bella's Greek house that had finished him at last. It was a cold house, he remembered. Bella had been generous, lending it for holidays, and Will and Coral had been there one chilly Easter.

Would Bella settle there now? It seemed unlikely that she would want to continue living like a gypsy on her own. But she was an Englishwoman; her two children lived in England, there was a boy, a doctor, younger than Will, and a girl younger still. Davey and Clare. Had she, in fact, somewhere to live in London, say, or out in the country, that she had never mentioned? Or sold, perhaps, when she married Silas?

Will was contrite suddenly. It seemed shameful to know so little *about* Bella. Especially when he liked her so much—well more than liked, *loved* her. She was a solid, rosy, happy woman, warm and loving. She had put her arms round Will and hugged him the first time she met him and he had quickly come to feel that she was the laughing young mother he had never had. He remembered saying to her, 'He's a lot older than you,' not jealous, exactly, but wanting to warn her. She had said, 'Oh, I'm used to old men. My dad died when I was two. You could say I'd been looking for him ever since and you might not be wrong.' And she had given one of her big, cheerful laughs. 'I can only say I've been very satisfied with the fathers I've found up to now.'

Will had wanted to ask her, 'What about bed?' It seemed a natural question: Bella seemed to him so openly and unfussily sexy and Silas—well, it was hard to think of Silas in bed with, making love to, anyone. And not just because of his age. But he didn't ask her.

Now, on his third brandy, scooping up the accompanying peanuts and cramming them into his mouth, he thought of Silas blaming a six-year-old for his mother's failing health, blaming him, perhaps, for what might have been the end of his own sexual life with his wife. Silas in his lusty fifties, disappointed with poor, worn-out Mother. If he had subsequently made other arrangements, he had always been discreet. And after Mother's death there had been no revelations, no sly introductions over a casual lunch meeting. *Ah, Will! I don't think you've met Sophie/ Antoinette/Margaret, have you?* No evidence that he had any further urges in that direction. When he began to book himself on the occasional luxury cruise around the Mediterranean, Alice had telephoned from

12

Maine to her sister in Yorkshire, her brother in London, in some agitation. Did they think *the old man was on the prowl*, was how she put it, a phrase that sounded mildly disgusting to Will's puritan ear. He was shocked that both Alice and Hannah appeared to take such an eager, lip-smacking pleasure in their elderly father's private adventures. Sitting in the kitchen of his tall terrace house in North London (Islington bordering on Hackney) he had envisaged his older sisters, cackling and rolling their eyes like the pair of smelly harpies he remembered from his early childhood, sniggering, nudging each other, at some innocent display of ignorance on his part (usually of a sexual nature), ugly sisters to his Cinderella. Objectively, when he was older and they had left home, he was able to recognise the useful part they had played in his upbringing, reading to him, playing Ludo and Monopoly on wet days, running beside him in the park while he was learning to ride his bicycle, taking on the role their mother was too tired (or unwilling) to play, but it had merely made him feel guilty because in spite of this recognition he still failed to love them. His overriding memories of them were physical and disagreeable: Alice, trapping his hot, screaming face in her armpit, her 'torture place' as a punishment, Hannah tickling him in the bath for the fun of seeing his little penis stand firm and calling Alice to laugh at him with her. 'Look at his nasty little secret! D'you think he knows what to do with it? Shall we show him?'

Huge, shiny faces, wet mouths, bright eyes, gleaming above him, shrouded in steam. And hateful humiliation compounded by uncontrollable tears and by great arms swooping down to console him, lift him out of the bath and cuddle him, shrouded in towels, against wet, smelly bulges of flesh. 'Poor little poppet, poor diddums, never mind, horrid Alice and Hannah.'

As Will called up this scene in the plane, disgust filled him, rising sour in his mouth. He shouldn't have had that last brandy. To compensate, he would refuse wine with the meal about to be served from the trolley that was making its way through from First Class to Club where he was seated. Although since food was the best antidote to alcohol, the best way to sober up, it would be easier to choke down the no doubt inedible fodder on offer with a glass of red wine. And he would need to be sober to face what awaited him once he landed at Athens; sober, not just to deal with his father's corpse but, more importantly, to console the sorrowing widow.

He thought about comforting Bella and a warm flush flowed agreeably through him. Bella would have to decide what should be done with her husband's body but he would be there to help her—must stay with her, at least until Davey or Clare, her doctor son or her

14

barrister daughter, arrived to take over. Fortunately this wasn't Coral's first baby and she had been quite calm, almost unmoved indeed, when he had kissed her goodbye in the hospital. Where Coral was concerned, calmness could be deceptive, cloaking anger, but on the whole in important things, at vital moments, she was entirely rational: certainly not the sort of woman to resent her husband flying to his father's deathbed.

Would Silas still be alive when he got there? And if alive, conscious? What would he say to his father? Or Silas to him? Presumably Bella would be there, so he had no need to worry about rehearsing suitable speeches. Bella was a skilful manager of difficult moments. And, as well as grief, there might be a modified joy on this sad occasion. Coral had always given birth quickly and easily. She might already have rung the hospital to say the child had been born. A new life to replace the old. Silas might even die happy.

The meal on his tray, tucking his napkin into his neck, nodding his acceptance at the bottle of claret poised above his glass, Will groaned with embarrassment. The idea of Silas entertaining such a notion was ludicrously indulgent. If he knew Will had played with it, even for a drunken instant, he would be contemptuous . . .

Though Bella would not be contemptuous, Will realised suddenly. It was just the kind of sweet, natural sentiment she would find comforting, the sense of life moving on. He saw himself putting his arms round her as they stood by Silas's body and murmuring into her ear that if the child were a boy they might call him Silas.

Perhaps Coral would allow it as a second name, though she would need some persuading. Mildly dyslexic, she had been forced to read *Silas Marner* at school and had hated the name ever since. It was lucky, Will thought, that she had let herself be conned into calling her father-in-law 'Daddy'. A joke on Silas's part that she had, surprisingly, taken seriously. Silas had always had a tendency to be sadistic towards women, Will considered. He could remember him raising an eyebrow at Alice who had appeared at some meal or other in a very new, very short mini skirt, and saying to Mother, 'Is that a wise garment, d'you think, for a young woman with legs like French furniture?' He had laughed as if he thought he had made a good joke and Will remembered, with shame now, that he had laughed too, to annoy Alice, although he had been unclear what his father had meant.

As the plane began its descent, looking out of the window and seeing the Acropolis far below, such a ridiculously *small* landmark to be so preposterously laden with history, Will wondered if Silas had been kinder to Bella. She had the advantage of him in some ways,

16

being younger. And Alice and Hannah had been right: he had been 'on the prowl'. He had picked up Bella on a cruise, sailing from Venice to Istanbul; rescued her, was how he had put it to Will, seeing her dancing in the arms of a man he was convinced was a gigolo. 'Dreadful creature, tight as a pea in a pod in a blazer and white trousers. And wearing a rug!'

Silas, whose own hair, though thinning now, still quite adequately covered his scalp, was contemptuous of unluckier men, either because they were bald or because they tried to conceal it. And when Bella explained that her partner was what was known as a 'Gentleman Host' of which there were several on this expensive ship (recruited to dance with the 'independently travelling ladies') Silas had been equally dismissive of their occupation. 'No job for a man who has any respect for himself.' 'But it is a *good* idea,' Bella had protested. 'All we poor widows who like dancing! Some of us haven't danced since our husbands died!'

Will could hear Bella saying this—'*we poor widows*'—speaking laughingly, not deprecatingly, apparently quite undismayed to be part of such doleful company. She was the most natural woman in the world, Will thought approvingly as the plane bumped on the tarmac and the Greeks among the passengers applauded the safe landing. Unselfconscious. Sweet. Open. Good.

It was probably why she had been able to be happy with Silas. Her sweet, open nature made her immune to his casual cruelties. But she must have been limited by him all the same. Silas didn't dance for one thing. And perhaps his daughters had been right about his shipboard intentions. There had been no more cruises after they married, no more chance for a Gentleman Host to put his arm around Bella's plump waist and twirl her round the floor.

How far had it gone? Had she ever taken one of them back to her cabin? The qualifications for the job were fairly specific. As well as being good dancers they had to be middle-aged and single; preferably widowed or divorced. The rules governing their social behaviour were strict. They were not supposed to dance twice with the same lady consecutively, or to sit down with her after the dance unless invited. But Bella was not the sort of woman to pay much attention to rules.

Would she be waiting for him at the airport? She knew the time of his plane. Oh, probably not. His mind might be racing, his pulse rate have risen, but that was the effect of brandy and an almost sleepless night on the heady emotional combination of a birth and a death on a normally placid getting-to-be-middle-aged man, not the prospect of an assignation. He should be ashamed. Lusting after his father's widow when his own wife was in the

18

labour ward. Lugging his overnight bag from the steps of the plane to the airport bus, Will said, 'Ha!' explosively, and then coughed, as if to clear some obstacle from his throat.

He hoped Silas had provided for Bella. There must be enough money but Silas rarely discussed his financial affairs. Unlike Mother. She had left her little fortune equally divided between her three children. *Little fortune* was what she had called the money her parents had left her: her father, an Edinburgh lawyer, her mother the only child of a prosperous Edinburgh draper. Neither had been pleased when she married Silas, in their view a cloddish young nobody from England, but they knew their family duty. No daughter of theirs should have to slave in the kitchen or iron her husband's shirts. How much they had left Mother originally to make her domestic life easy was a mystery to her son and her daughters who each received twenty-eight thousand pounds when she died; a useful amount but not quite the sum they had been led to expect from the awed, whispered pride with which Mother had so frequently mentioned it. Silas had made no comment on his children's inheritance except once to Will. 'That'll set you up a bit. Buy yourself a decent suit.' Will had replied, rather haughtily, that he thought it would be more sensible to put the money towards a down payment on a house. He had his eye on one in north Islington. (And

19

on Coral as well, but at that time she had been too uncertain a prospect to mention to anyone. Particularly not to his father.)

Will supposed Silas would leave a fair bit. The way he'd been living, though not extravagant (he never travelled other than economy class on a plane, what would be the point when whatever you paid you arrived at the same time?) was pleasantly comfortable. He stayed in decent hotels, ate and drank well, hired cars (for Bella to drive) whenever he wanted to. He had once said to Will, one of the few times he had talked to him about money, that it cost less to live as he did than to run a house or an apartment. With a house, apart from the relentless bills, rates, fuel, food, furniture, there was the *capital lying idle*. He had lowered his voice respectfully. 'You've tied up a sum, say, four hundred thousand. At ten per cent, evened out for the argument, that's forty thousand pounds going to waste every year. Can't use it, can't touch it.' A house was a tax-free investment, Will had pointed out, whereas the income from the same value in shares would be taxable, but Silas had smiled. Since Mother had died and he had sold up all he owned in this country, spent a full year abroad, and then never more than ninety days a year in the United Kingdom, he had not paid tax anywhere.

Of course, if his father *hadn't* made proper arrangements for Bella, he would have to talk it over with Hannah and Alice, make certain that a proper family rearrangement, or whatever they called it, was sorted out. Even if Bella had money of her own, she deserved a reasonable reward for the five and a half years she had taken care of Silas, care that would have fallen on his children had she not been there. If Hannah and Alice didn't agree he would have to stand up for Bella, fight her corner against his sisters, those greedy harpies! Fired up with indignation in prospect, Will stamped his feet waiting in line to shuffle through Immigration, strode through the baggage hall, leather carry-on thumping his hip bone, through Customs, out through the automatic glass doors, shaky-legged, heart thumping, diving into the chaos of the welcoming, jostling, flower-clutching Athenian crowd, eagerly searching for Bella.

And instead, saw his octogenarian father; a broken, skinny, bent-shouldered old crow, head thrust forward, leaning on his two sticks, waiting . . .

*   *   *

Silas, in his hundredth year, in the dining room of his London club, is talking to his daughter-in-law about his son Will, not about Bella: 'No stamina, I'm afraid. His age, he ought to have thrown off a bit of flu. Not his heart, I hope?'

It had been heart that had finished Bella. 'I

21

had no idea!' Silas had said to Will. 'Such a well-fleshed, healthy woman, who'd have thought it? And she knew, of course. That she might go any time. So her boy, Davey, told me afterwards. But she hadn't told me. Didn't want to worry me, Davey said. But it leaves a sour taste, you know, a sour taste . . .'

Now Silas's forehead reddens—with outrage, Coral assumes—as he remembers his dead wife's deception. But he lowers his voice to the same hushed tone he employs to speak about money 'Or *cancer*? Something serious!'

'Pneumonia is serious,' Coral says coldly. Then relents. He is an old man, after all. She smiles. 'He'll be all right, though. He wouldn't want you to worry.'

She wonders if he hears the echo: all these people keeping things from him. But he only shakes his head and sighs. 'I'm afraid Will won't make old bones,' he says.

CHAPTER TWO

Too pleased with herself, that girl, Silas thinks, steadily masticating a thick slice of Aberdeen Angus beef, the club's best offering from the trolley on Saturdays, glancing slyly at his daughter-in-law who had ordered partridge instead, even though he had told her it was bound to be frozen. As if she had her name up

22

in lights all over town instead of bit parts, blink-and-she's-gone. Sitting there, head on one side, hacking at a little bird, all bones and leather, wouldn't admit she'd made a mistake, smiling away, ought to wear something round her neck, half a mind to tell her it's getting scraggy . . .

Silas doesn't dislike Coral. Truth is, much of the time, he doesn't see her. Or, rather, he sees *through her* to his adored sister, Molly. Coral fades to spectral transparency; through her, behind her, Molly blooms, takes on rosy life. Molly Mudd, actress.

Molly would be a hundred and seven years old now. Very old bones if she'd lived. Born in the early nineties, died a few months after the end of the war, the Great War, World War One, singing her heart out in Collins's music hall up in Islington, not all that far from Will's present shoddy little house, jobbing builder's Georgian, why on earth did the stupid boy buy it? Slum property. Worth a lot now, going on for three-quarters of a million, so they say, bet they wouldn't get it, though. Molly had rented a room for a while looking over the canal, the Grand Union, had to keep the window closed night and day, winter and summer, stench from the water, flies from the rubbish floating down from the lock, filthy language from the bargees. And the rats. More rats in the street than people, Molly said, she was glad to get out of it when she teamed up with that man—

what'shisname?— and the child. They had a great act going, the three of them, did well enough to rent a nice little house in Walthamstow, but then the child died of the Spanish flu and the man lost heart and Molly was on her own again, no money, no one to help her, only her gift, that wonderful voice. She sang in the music halls, sentimental ballads, scraping a living. A waste—she could have been a great comic actress. They had thought so at the Royal Academy of Dramatic Art where she had studied for three terms, on a scholarship. Aunt, Geneva Martha Mudd, their father's older sister, the teacher in Swaffham, had paid her living expenses—not lavishly, just enough to stop her starving—and her niece's progress report was sent to her at the end of the year.

Quite our best vulgar comedian!

That was what brought her down. This girl, Coral, his daughter-in-law sitting opposite him, daintily nibbling the last of the flesh off the partridge's skeleton, has no idea, none at all, how lucky she is, how easy her life . . .

Silas says, his voice rough with jealousy, 'Did I ever tell you about the report Molly got from the Royal Academy of Dramatic Art at the end of her first year? They said she was a brilliant vulgar comedian. Of course, Aunt wouldn't stand for that. She didn't see it was praise. She had expected Molly to be a great actress like Sarah Siddons. Stopped her

24

allowance at once. Poor Molly. She had to go on the halls, took up with that man and his child . . .'

Silas frowns. He is being unfair to Aunt. Molly hadn't blamed Aunt, after all. No one decently could. Aunt had taken them on, her brother's three motherless children, Molly and Silas and Baby May, when he lost his good job in London and went to America (ran away, to Aunt's mind) and she was determined to make the best job she could of them, see they were educated and respectably launched on the world.

Coral says, 'I think Pippa may find her feet on the stage. She's joined the university theatre club, auditioned for several parts, no luck *so far*, but if she's got your sister's genes as well as mine she may be in with a chance!'

She is smiling kindly. Once Coral has started talking about her children, Silas reckons he is safe. He doesn't have to strain to listen in case an answer is required. His grandchildren do not concern him and all he need sustain is an interested expression. Behind it, he can let his own thoughts ramble comfortably.

*   *   *

He is thinking of Molly. Of Aunt. Of Aunt's brother, his father. Henry Mudd had told his children that he was going to America to make

25

the family fortune, and for several years he did send money home, American dollars folded into dense letters in minute writing, rapturously describing this beautiful new country, the wonderful opportunities open and waiting for everyone who had the slightest spark of energy and imagination. His present well-paid work on the railways was only a beginning. Then he met a distant cousin (of whom Aunt had never heard and made it clear she didn't believe in) who encouraged him to invest his wages in a saloon in one of the Gold Rush shanty towns that were springing up all over California, and after that the letters grew less frequent and the dollars ceased. He had left his children when Molly was twelve, Silas four, and May only a baby; he came home penniless thirteen years later, an old, broken man, a stranger to his two surviving children, fit for nothing but stoking the boiler at the Methodist chapel. He was paid a pittance, which he handed over to Aunt, but the job didn't last and he was dependent on his sister as his children had been.

And Silas, who should have been able to take care of Molly, his sister, his darling, had signed up as a trainee mechanic in the Royal Flying Corps a year before he had needed to, an insignificant cog in a stupid war. That is, it seems stupid to Silas from where he stands now: all those dead young men, the cream of a generation skimmed off, wasted, and to what end?

Nowadays, when he visits his past, Silas asks questions of himself more often than he answers them. Why was it that Molly, the flower of the flock, that beautiful girl with smooth white shoulders and a face like a rose, should have been the one falling lifeless on the stage of the music hall while her adoring brother, awkward in his stiff, creaky uniform, sat in the audience, unable to help her?

Heart, they said. Molly had a weak heart, just like Bella. Aunt had paid for the funeral, for four black horses with plumes and brass handles to the coffin, and the flowers that filled Swaffham churchyard were tribute from a town that respected Aunt and had loved Molly. Girls who had played with her, travelled daily on the Norwich train to school with her, boys who had danced with her in the Assembly Rooms, chandeliers tinkling, floor swaying under their thumping feet, sobbed in the church; men and women who had watched her grow up stood straight-backed and stern-faced until the Vicar's voice faltered as he spoke of *our golden girl.* The rest of his eulogy was drowned in the trumpeting of blown noses.

Silas had not wept. He had fixed his gaze on the flying wooden angels in the roof and counted backwards from a thousand, which was a trick Molly had taught him when he was a little boy and inclined to be lachrymose. He counted steadily, silently, and looked to his future. He would be out of uniform soon and Aunt wanted him to go to Cambridge; she was certain he would get a scholarship, her clever, hard-working nephew. He was used to obeying Aunt, but he wanted his freedom. Besides, he had to take care of his father whom he called 'Dad', to please him, but thought of as Henry, and of Aunt too, who had suddenly and quite unexpectedly grown older and frailer, the pair of them living together in moderate harmony in Aunt's cottage on the London Road with the long garden behind it, an undisciplined tangle of gooseberry bushes and Michaelmas daisies, and Aunt's pet chicken ruling the roost from a comfortable cushion by the fire in the kitchen. Silas didn't want to live there with them, sleeping in the back bedroom, which was no more than a cupboard two steps down from a bigger bedroom, and where the bulky tin bath, hooked on the back of the door, left just enough room for a narrow bed. He had slept there long enough, all his boyhood, kept awake by Aunt's snores and groans. She had suffered from catarrh and bad dreams; one terrifying night when Silas was twelve or so, he had woken to hear her screaming, 'Don't shoot, in the name of God don't shoot me.' And when, fearfully, he had peeped through a crack in the door he had seen her sitting bolt upright, wild-eyed, her hand at her throat.

He had been at the grammar school then and until he left to join up he had worked

Saturdays in the ironmonger's shop on the Market Square. Arnold Pepys, who owned it and three other shops in the small towns around Norwich, had said there would be a regular job for him when he came back from the war. It wasn't what he had hoped for, some of Aunt's ambition had stoked his imagination with grander prospects, but he saw now that it would do to begin with and not a bad beginning either. He enjoyed working with hard, useful objects, tools with a purpose, and he had always liked the smell of the shop: predominantly the smell of tarred string.

Arnold Pepys was delighted. He was getting on in years, the war had tired him, and Geneva Martha Mudd was well respected in the town. To have her smart young nephew working for him, at his beck and call, boosted his own social position to something more than a shopkeeper. He had no children of his own; he needed a young man to train up to manage the business. He saw himself handing over the reins and inviting young Silas to dinner on Saturdays to give an account of his stewardship. A decent roast dinner and one of his wife's good puddings, and looking at the books afterwards over a pipe and a glass of port. He sent Silas to manage the Wymondham shop, quite small, but serving a broad-based farming community, and found him lodgings with the widow of a clergyman to whom he delivered regular supplies of firewood and paraffin and of whom he was discreetly enamoured.

Silas was happy. The old man was to pay him two pounds five shillings a week, well above the odds for those days and enough to pay the widow for his board and lodging, give Aunt ten shillings a week to help look after Henry, and leave him a bit over for saving towards his grand future and fun. Not much of that living with Aunt, fun coming low down on her list of priorities, and Silas, to be honest, wasn't quite sure what he meant by it either, except whatever it was he yearned for it with a deep, aching longing.

A good many boys he remembered from the grammar school were no longer around. Some of them, among them his closest friend, the gamekeeper's son, had been killed in the war. Others had found jobs in Norwich, or further afield, as far away as London. It seemed to Silas that those who had stayed behind were the dullards, content to be agricultural labourers or domestic servants and only interested in getting drunk and mauling girls—many of whom, to Silas's amazement, seemed to have changed from the prim, untouchable creatures he remembered from before the war, and become not only willing but eager. Lovers' Lane, a narrow grass road between high hedges, once a pleasant evening stroll for what Aunt's influence had conditioned him to think of as 'respectable' couples, now echoed, as darkness thickened, to happy groans and sighs. Silas, both shocked and envious, told himself he wouldn't want a girl who gave herself too readily. Or not to others, anyway. He wanted (though he didn't know it) a girl he could take home to Aunt.

Which meant (and this he surely knew) a refined and educated girl with some class about her, certainly several notches higher than his own, to compensate for being a motherless boy with an incompetent old father and a sister who, however beautiful and beloved, had only been able to make a living by singing on the music halls; a family, in fact, who had only been redeemed, if not actually kept out of the workhouse, by his good, hard-working aunt.

*   *   *

He did better than even Aunt could have expected. The Edinburgh lawyer's daughter, staying with a cousin in a small manor house on the Norwich Road, attended Swaffham church one Sunday and sat, with her cousin and her cousin's husband, in the pew immediately in front of Silas, his father and his aunt. Her fair hair was clustered on her fragile neck and, as she twisted round her lifted head to look at the flying angels of the roof, she presented her pretty profile—delicate nose, soft, pouting lips—to the young man behind her, and his generalised, vaguely visceral longings became specific, focused. Aunt, it turned out, had given private lessons to the cousin's husband (who was rather dim) to prepare him for his common-entrance examination some fifteen years ago, and after the service was over it was natural for introductions to be made, and for Aunt to walk ahead down the church path, chatting to her ex-pupil and his wife, while her nephew and Effie Ogilvie followed slowly, gazing at each other.

If the cousin's husband had been sharper-witted nothing might have come of it. But he was bored with having his wife's attention taken up by her young cousin and was only too happy for Aunt to take her off his hands and home to tea with Silas. Aunt's almost innocent collusion—lace cloth on the round table in the best front room, silver teapot, fine bone china—stopped at leaving them alone together in the parlour, but she was happy for Silas to walk Effie home after the meal was finished and didn't ask, when he returned much later, why he had been away so long. Nor warn him that a shop assistant, however favoured by the owner, might not be quite the sort of match Effie's parents envisaged for their only daughter.

Perhaps Aunt was a romantic at heart. Or a brave woman in advance of her time, refusing to be cowed by any rigid ideas of class structure dependent on money or birth. Education was her template; education and only education was the mould, the model by which a person should be judged. 'Get yourself educated,' was one of her injunctions to all her pupils. 'Never lose sight of your own importance,' was another.

Of course it is also possible that she simply had an eye for the main chance. To her dismay, Silas had decided against Cambridge. Marrying up, in Aunt's view, was the next best thing. But the odds are that like everyone else she had a mixture of motives, some elevated, some venal.

Nothing complicated about Silas's instincts, impulses, however. He was just drowned in love.

*   *   *

Coral says, 'Daddy?'

She is still smiling at him. Has she been sitting there all the time with that sweet, indulgent smile? They have obviously each ordered dessert from the trolley; there is a strawberry left on his plate, and the remains of some chocolate pudding on Coral's.

Coral says, 'Do you want cheese? They've got what looks like a very good Stilton.'

Silas looks at her. She is quite solid; there is no sign of Molly lurking behind her. Has he drifted off while she was talking? How long for?

He touches his napkin to the corners of his mouth in case he is dribbling and says, 'Has Will done the table plan yet? He's not too ill for that, is he? I think I'll have young Clare on my right. She's got a good clear voice. She'll let me know what's going on.'

CHAPTER THREE

Coral, hunched in her coat against the bitter cold, puts her head down as she rounds the corner and advances on the hospital steps, watching her feet on the ice. She doesn't see the man until she is almost upon him. She hears a small sound—a grunt, a sigh?—and looks up.

He is sitting in his wheelchair at the top of the steps, just outside the glass doors of the hospital, a tartan blanket, white and green and black, covering the lower part of his body—if there is any lower part: the blanket looks empty where his legs ought to be. From the waist upwards, his whole upper body is bare. His white chest is broad and firm and unblemished, his arms strong and muscular. His full black beard, which gives him the look of someone who ought to be clothed in some kind of majestic, or at least formal attire, makes his nakedness even more startling.

34

He is smoking a cigarette. A refugee from the harsh rule of the hospital. But *naked*? In this freezing weather?

He looks at Coral briefly, indifferently, and then fixes his gaze straight ahead. He has small, sharp eyes like dark, polished buttons. To say something, anything—such as what? Can I help you? Are you all right? Would you like me to get you a blanket?—seems an impertinence. His entire stance is so confident, even arrogant. And he doesn't look cold.

Another man, standing, and fully clothed, long dark cashmere coat, expensive-looking dark green velvet cap, is patiently holding open the heavy glass door for her. Their eyes meet. Coral thinks his gleam with amusement. The oddity of the naked man in the wheelchair? Or her obvious discomfiture? She smiles her thanks as she walks past him into the fiercely hot air of the hospital, then turns expectantly. But although he nods, politely returning her smile, he says nothing. He presses the bell for the lift, which opens at once. Coral enters, preceding him, and turns again to interrogate him with widening eyes, an arched eyebrow. Surely there can be no mistaking her theatrically enquiring expression? But he still remains silent. His forefinger hovers over the numbered buttons. Which floor? Coral whispers, 'Four, please. Thank you.' But nothing more. It is as if a spell, or some kind of shameful conspiracy, holds them.

The lift stops. The doors squeal open. Coral waits, willing this stranger to speak. His silence seems to invalidate what she has seen. *If* she has seen it. She is already—not doubting exactly, just somehow feeling certainty slipping away from her. But he only regards her gravely, raises his cap half an inch from his forehead and is gone down the corridor, the skirts of his coat swirling around him.

Will is in bed in a side ward, propped on pillows, transparent plastic mask over his nose and mouth, breathing through a nebuliser. He lifts three fingers in greeting. Three more minutes, and he'll be off the machine and able to speak to her.

She takes off her coat, hangs it from the hook on the back of the door and sits, conscientiously straight-backed, on the uncomfortable slippery chair provided for visitors, skirt smoothed beneath her, ankles neatly crossed. She is aware of Will watching her dispose herself in the manner she knows he thinks of as actressy, and it makes her selfconscious. Although she had intended to tell him about the naked smoker, she cannot think now how to express the odd sense of displacement that had seized and inhibited her. And superstition creeps in. Had it been an ill omen?

She says, 'It's Arctic out, darling. You're in the best place, though I don't expect you to

36

think so. Not just the weather. Your pa has been playing one of his games with me. Making mischief. When he isn't drifted off into an old man's sleep. Tell you later. More immediate, he's fussing about the seating plan. He'll have to have the club chairman's wife on his right, so he says, and he wants Bella's Clare on his left. That's going to make trouble with your sisters, isn't it? I don't suppose Alice will mind, not too much, anyway, but Hannah will. I mean, her two, Jane and Paul, *live* in London . . .'

Will pulls the mask from his face, turns off the nebuliser and says, slowly and patiently, 'He's not inviting any of the grandchildren. He said that from the beginning. Too many, have to draw the line somewhere, he said. Is that unreasonable? He'd have to ask all Alice's frightful brood, which would not only be a terrible test of endurance for the rest of us but would almost certainly mean paying their fare from the States. That's the main thing. I got the impression that he wouldn't mind asking our kids, well, at least Pippa and Rory, and Hannah's, but that he felt he'd have to ask all the grandchildren if he asked one of them. That would mean an extra eight places and the room he's booked in the club isn't that big. I think he's already at maximum, anyway.

'But Hannah's two are about the same age as Clare! That's what I *meant*. I think Clare is actually younger than Jane and Paul, isn't she?

Davey may be older, but only a year or two.'

'They are Bella's *children*, my love. His step-children. Our generation to his mind. They both have proper jobs. Proper clothes. And they don't wear nose rings.'

'I don't think that's how your sisters will see it. Hannah won't, certainly. You know Hannah.'

Will says, sharper now, 'Bella's children have done more for Father, seen much more *of* him, and he of them, than any of his own grandchildren except perhaps Dinkie. And she's only seen him more often than the others because she's still a child at home, and usually around when he comes to see us.'

'But putting Clare next to him! Bella's daughter, his stepdaughter, when he has two daughters of his own flesh and blood. Hannah will be *insulted.*'

'That's Hannah's problem. Perhaps when you get to Father's age you reckon you can get away with insulting your daughters.'

'I simply don't want *trouble*, that's all. Unpleasantness.'

'Unlike the rest of us who are itching for murder and mayhem?' Will laughs and coughs harshly, holding his side.

'Oh, *darling.* Does it still hurt when you breathe?'

'Only when I laugh.'

'I didn't mean to make you laugh. I didn't mean to be funny'

'You weren't in the least funny. I made myself laugh.'

'Nothing subtle about your sense of humour.'

'No. Sorry.'

*   *   *

Will is genuinely apologetic. The truth, he suspects, is that Coral is insulted herself and rightly, perhaps. She has been more attentive to the old man than his own daughters; these last years, it has always been Coral who drove him around when he was in London, shopped for his underwear in Marks and Spencer and in Selfridges for the delicacies, the salt beef slices, the jars of red caviar he likes to keep in the fridge in his room at the club. Well, she has time to spare at the moment. Since she was written out of that soap. That upset her, but it is a blessing in disguise for professional reasons. So she bravely insists, anyway. Playing a derelict pensioner with bad legs isn't what she aspires to. She is still serious about her work. She might well have expected to sit next to the old man at his centenary dinner. Though she would never say so.

Of course, Clare is like her mother. Rosy and firm, if not quite so plump. The same wild, soft, tangled hair. Bella—only Bella much younger. That's why Silas wants her next to him. The pleasure of warm, sweet-smelling young flesh within reach of his hand. And no wonder.

Will resists the temptation to point this out to Coral. Instead, he says, 'You never really liked Bella, did you?'

She seems simply surprised. Instead of hurt—as perhaps he'd intended? 'Not as wholeheartedly as you did, anyone could see you were dotty about her. I wondered sometimes how your father felt about that.'

Will sees her frown suddenly. What now? What is lurking behind that pale, high, calm forehead. Is she wondering if Bella could have been Silas's mistress all along? How had Silas arranged it? The apparently dutiful husband of a sick wife, he had been at home fairly consistently as far as Will could remember. Out in the evenings, occasionally, there must have been opportunities. But a second family, concealed from the first, run in tandem?

No. Rubbish. Such a fantasy would never cross Coral's sensible mind. It was his feverish imagination entirely. What did they call it? Toxic confusion. The effect of the illness. When he had first been carried into this side ward, it had seemed to him that the yellow paint of the hospital wall was shimmering and dissolving into an eighteenth-century rural scene as it might have been painted by Watteau, but shifting and changing, sailing clouds in the sky, nymphs and shepherds dancing, round young limbs gleaming. Well, he'd had a temperature of forty degrees. He had tried to tell Coral, or maybe one of the nurses, but the words had been inaccessible, he couldn't even formulate them in his mind, let alone speak them. And the Watteau had been gone by the morning.

Coral says, 'I suppose it was the money that changed things for your sisters. Hardly calculated to make them more kindly inclined towards Bella.'

'Only in retrospect. She was dead before they knew. And I was against telling them, if you remember.'

'No, I don't. You were *frightened* of telling them. *That's* what I remember. You came back from Athens and there I was, nursing Dinkie, and you barely looked at her, your new daughter, before you started waving your arms about and trotting out umpteen reasons why you shouldn't tell Hannah and Alice that their loving father had put a vast lump of his capital into a trust for Bella, with her as the sole beneficiary in case they decided to come back to England and settle, and now she had carelessly gone and died he couldn't get at the money. I never understood why, mind you, but you know how I am about money.'

'I'm not sure I understood either. Not then and not now. Just that it was tax efficient and safe from death duties. Bella could make inter-vivos gifts on his behalf, she was more likely to live another seven years than he was. Fair

41

enough if he'd gone first, as he'd expected to, the plan had included her making a new will, in favour of his children as well as her own, but they had been waiting to do that until they had talked to Bella's Greek lawyer. I did tell you at the time, I can't remember the details now. Something to do with Bella's house, Greek property law being so complicated. But when they did go to Athens, it was to the hospital and the arms of the Reaper. And you're quite right, I didn't want to tell my greedy sisters. Death seemed preferable. Mind you, only child as you are, you can have no idea . . .'

They smile at each other.

Coral says, 'I've learned from you. Watching and listening.'

* * *

Hannah and Alice had seemed harmless enough to her, both when she first met them, and later. She had been told that Alice was tremendously clever, which had disconcerted her to begin with, but Alice's cleverness, being scientific, hardly counted. Besides, she was so small and delicate, like a frail child. And she had no interest in theatre. Hannah, twice her sister's size, might have been voluptuous as a young woman, but by the time Coral had met her she was encased in rolls of flesh so soft and ponderous that they seemed only contained by her clothes; as if when she took them off, she might deliquesce into a shapeless heap of blubber. She is still fat. She is married to a law professor, a refugee from Berlin she met at Oxford in the forties when she went up to read modern languages; except for a couple of years in the sixties when he was seconded to Harvard, they lived on Boar's Hill most of their married life. Now Julius is retired from teaching, they have a house in the Yorkshire Dales where they breed very pretty sheep, white with black faces—a strange occupation to Coral's mind, but it seems to make them both happy.

Coral finds both sisters agreeable women, but dull. It amazes her how terrified of them Will seems to be.

Talking to Hannah that evening, he had been white as chalk. Sitting on the couch, cuddling warm, milky Dinkie, she could easily hear her older sister-in-law's furious quacking as he held the receiver at a pained distance from his ear. Hannah, demanding that Will call upon Bella's children *immediately* to determine what was to be done. They would have to agree to relinquish their inheritance, part of it, anyway. And what bothered poor Will, as it would, was not this request, which was in itself moderately reasonable given the circumstances—or at least not *unreasonable*— but the distasteful prospect of having to put it in person to Davey and Clare to whom he was bound to appear venal; greedily determined to grab back money that had, perfectly properly, been given by a loving husband to their beloved, and only just deceased, mother.

Though it is unlikely that either Davey or Clare will have thought on those lines for a minute. They are both models of diligent public service, living equally decorously their private lives, the general practitioner with a wife and twin daughters, the barrister sharing the mortgage on a loft conversion in Wapping with an old friend who is the head of a local comprehensive school.

Anyway, why couldn't Silas have told them himself what he had done? If it worried him? He had left himself enough to live on, Will had explained—rather mysteriously it seemed to Coral: she had not thought this was the point. Certainly it was no argument to put to Hannah, not even to Alice who, unlike her sister, affected to despise inherited wealth and all personal property and, anyway, earned enough to keep herself, her young lover, and her four children (none of them at home now, but none of them earning a regular wage and all needing subventions) on the right side of the bread line.

Alice is a geneticist, the leader of a team in her laboratory in Maine; her international recognition comes from her work on the cloning of the H3a transplantation antigen gene. What this means is as mysterious to Coral as her father-in-law's attitude to money,

44

but Alice had once tried to explain it and Coral, who is a good study, has filed this job description in her mind, apparently permanently.

Coral remembers saying to Will around this time that she sometimes felt her actor's brain was clogged with such a vast store of useless information that only the arrival of senility would wipe it clear. That was when she could still say what she liked to Will without the shiver of trepidation that sometimes afflicts her now. When had she started to feel that whenever she spoke he was judging her?

She says, 'Well, you stood up to Hannah.'

'Cowardice. Procrastination. Not wanting to appear grasping. Besides, I was sure it wasn't what Father wanted. He preferred to forget it, put it behind him. He only told me because he was so angry with Bella for dying and spoiling his plans that he had to tell someone. The next time he mentioned it, the only other time, he said, however it had turned out, he was glad he had done that for Bella. She had nothing of her own, only the Greek house, and a smallish annuity. And a married woman ought to have independent means, he said.'

Coral hesitates. 'Hannah asked me, last time we spoke on the phone, if I knew what Bella's children had *done with the money.* Lowering her voice to a sinister baritone as if she thought they might be engaged in some illicit activity. Spying, or smuggling drugs. I said I had no idea. I don't think she believed me. Perhaps she wondered if you had actually come to some arrangement with them that cut her out, and Alice, but worked to your advantage!'

She sees, with amusement, that Will looks appalled. She says, 'I told Hannah that whatever Davey and Clare had done with the money their mother had left them, it was none of her business. I said that instead of resenting them in this paranoid fashion, she should be grateful to them for the trouble they've taken over Daddy since Bella died, seeing him at least once a week when he's in London, running errands for him and taking him out, especially since neither she nor Alice seem to have either the time or the inclination to bother about him all that often, or not much beyond the occasional postcard or telephone call.'

Will closed his eyes, apparently in pain. 'Did you have to?'

'No.'

He opened his eyes and looked at her reproachfully.

She says, 'I don't suppose I upset her, she's got a hide like an alligator. And it will give her a grievance to work on, get her in training for this jolly family occasion coming up any minute. Do you suppose she quarrels with her nice husband? Or is he *too* nice? So she doesn't get enough of that sort of exercise.'

46

Will groans.

Coral says, 'I'm glad I'm an only child. I suppose we are lucky our children seem to get on. At least, when they see each other. Look at it this way. For once you won't be first in the line of fire. Hannah will be angry with *me*.'

'You are becoming coarse in your middle years,' Will says sternly. 'It doesn't become you.'

Coral cannot tell from his tone or expression whether this is a joke or not. She decides to smile. 'You're a lot better, aren't you? Yesterday you were so saintly, I was afraid you were about to fall off your perch. I expect you'll be back in the main ward tomorrow so you'll have company. Would you mind if I went to Brighton tomorrow for a couple of days? Well, a week, actually, but I'll only need to stay the night at the beginning. When we're under way I can catch the late train home and visit you in the mornings. It's, well, the RSC have asked me to play Gertrude, take over for this bit of the tour, Judy has to have the week off and Greg—do you remember Greg?—thought of me . . .'

She can feel her pulse racing. She laughs. 'I suppose you'll think I'm silly to be excited. Like a teenage understudy getting her chance . . .'

Will says, 'It's wonderful, darling. You'll be a wonderful Gertrude. I only wish I could get down to see you. What about Dinkie?'

'She can stay with her friend. That family in

47

Thornhill Road. I'm not sure you—'

'Merivale? Angela Merivale? Tall girl . . . Oh, I am so very glad, darling.'

Coral says, 'I'll be going down tomorrow quite early.' She smiles at Will, grateful that he seems so unaffectedly pleased. Though what had she expected? She wants to give him something back, to reward him. Perhaps make him laugh?

She says, 'I forgot to tell you. There was this woman on the bus. She was wearing peasant rig and what looked like exceptionally heavy men's shoes. A left shoe on each foot. Everyone managed to avoid her gaze except me. She caught my eye like the Ancient Mariner and told me her tale. I'll spare you the whole of it. The gist was, she had eaten a corned-beef sandwich from what she called Down the Homeless. And it had made her sick. Terrible sick to her stomach, she said. Then at the end she vomited up a hard lump of something bright orange. You'll never guess what. Half a Rawlplug. She said, did I think she ought to go to the hospital. The other half might still be inside her. I said I wouldn't worry if I were her. That there had probably only been half a Rawlplug in the first place, somehow chopped up in the corned beef. In Argentina, or wherever it came from . . .'

'Good heavens,' Will says. He yawns, and smiles. 'Why didn't you take a taxi?'

'Oh, Will,' she says. '*Will* . . .' She sighs and

stands up. She says, brightly, 'Saving my hard-earned money. As your father says, a married woman ought to have her independence.'

CHAPTER FOUR

'I suppose you've thought of that,' Silas's prospective father-in-law had said. 'I suppose you know we've got money.'

'No, sir. It's not my business to know anything of that sort. All I know is, I love Effie and I want to marry her. She's done me the honour of accepting me.'

Effie's lawyer father, a Writer to the Signet, had not asked him to sit down. He sat, himself, behind a wide, polished desk, the light from the window behind him turning his grey hair into a nimbus of silver and leaving his long, bony face in shadow. Silas could not see the expression in his eyes. He wondered how his own appearance stood up to the cold Edinburgh glare. He had shaved at the station, washed, slicked his hair tidy, but his good suit was rumpled from a night sitting up in the train. Aunt had been right. He should have packed his suit and travelled in his everyday clothes. But he had been uncertain whether there would be a place to change in the station. And he had wanted to set out smart and confident from the beginning. That was something Molly had taught him. 'Feel good about yourself, that's the important thing. It gives you a glow. Other people will sense it without knowing what it is makes you different.' But he had looked at himself in the gents' at the station and felt his confidence dwindle. Swaffham-smart was not Edinburgh-smart. And there was a stain that he was sure had not been there earlier, on the lapel of his jacket.

He concentrated on Effie and gathered his courage. She was the prize of his life, his purpose, his future. He had been working five years for Arnold Pepys, rising at five in the morning, in bed by eleven six days a week, Saturday evenings dining with Pepys and his hard-breathing old wife in the best front room that smelt of leaking gas mantles, coal dust and sour elderly bodies, forcing down the blackened overcooked beef and the heavy, dry pudding that passed for a celebration dinner in their household. The miserably small glass of port that came afterwards, poured by Arnold Pepys with a great air of benevolence, was not much compensation for the dreadful meal, although Silas did enjoy the inspection of 'the books' that accompanied it. He had found he had a head for figures and could quickly see where certain lines were not paying their way in relation to the space they occupied. One kind of lawn-mower, for example, that appeared to sell better than a smaller and cheaper model was in fact less profitable because it took up more room, had to be delivered by carrier, and needed repairs and spare parts much more often. It took several Saturdays to convince Arnold Pepys but once he had grasped the principle he was delighted with Silas and congratulated himself on his acumen in employing him. 'I knew that young man would be good for business, Hepzibah,' he confided to Mrs Pepys, as he settled down on the feather mattress in the brass bed where they had slept every night of their married life, and embarked on the self-flattering round-up with which he liked to end his day. 'There's not many would have spotted him, I can tell you, but I've always had an eye for a smart young man. It's not easy, mind. You have to be a judge of character and that's born in you, not acquired. It's not something you can be taught. You know he's offered to take the Wymondham shop off my hands? Well, I've half a mind to let him have it at a good price. I won't be going on for ever, Hep, and it'ud please me to see the good business I've set up passing into safe custody.'

'He's got his eye on that Ogilvie girl, the one that visits family on the Norwich Road,' his sleepy wife answered. 'Comes to stay every summer, down from Scotland. Bit of a madam, some say, but she's got pretty ways with her. She was in the post office that time I dropped my purse, coins rolling everywhere, and she picked them all up for me straight away, sweet as honey. Old Mrs Greengrass saw them kissing in the churchyard, disgraceful place to choose she said, but I said to her, nothing wrong, it's just a young person's nature. It won't hurt the dead.'

She was snoring within a minute. Arnold Pepys, who disapproved of gossip, was gratified in this instance. If his protégé was making a play for one of the gentry on the Norwich Road he had been right to pick him out in the first place. A young man who would go far. Was it possible that one of the family, not wanting the Ogilvie girl to marry a mere shop *assistant*, was putting up the money to buy the Wymondham shop, make him a *shop-owner*? There was the old aunt, but although she bore herself grandly—gave herself airs, some might say—he doubted if she had money.

He was wrong. Aunt had 'a bit put by'. Years of making do and mending, and two unexpected windfalls: a couple of pupils who had each left her a small but useful sum and then died before marriage and children could weaken their sense of gratitude to an old teacher, one killed at the battle of the Somme, the other, like the poor child in Molly Mudd's musical-hall act, dead of the Spanish flu. 'I'll pay you back, every penny,' Silas had promised. 'Neither a borrower nor a lender be,' Aunt had answered, adding, with sombre emphasis, 'Besides, I'm not likely to be needing money much longer.'

He paid back Aunt within the year, long before her graveyard forebodings were fulfilled. By the time he travelled to Edinburgh to face his future father-in-law, he was not only the owner of a flourishing ironmongery shop but free of debt. The glorious six weeks each summer when Effie came to her cousin, he had risen two hours earlier to get his work done, and by the time she went back to Scotland the memory she took with her to nourish her love through the winter was of a romantically haggard young lover, all bones and hollows, dark eyes on fire with exhaustion.

Frustration, too. Effie had been seventeen when they met, six years younger than Silas, and her youth, the fact she was still at school, made her untouchable to his reverent mind. Or only touchable within limits. The second summer, to his terrified delight, she took his hands and placed them on her breasts; she would have pressed herself against him, had he allowed it. But he was afraid she would notice his erection and he thought she was too young to understand what she was doing; that her unexpected enthusiasm for love-making, for tickling his ear with her tongue, for wriggling her round little bottom when she sat on his lap, was innocent, schoolgirlish gambolling, and it was up to him, so much older, to respect that innocence. He told himself that the time was so short, and he was often so tired, that just to be in love, to walk hand in hand, to kiss—and not only in the churchyard, though that was their usual meeting place, midway between Aunt's cottage and the manor house on the Norwich Road—was sweetness enough. Besides, he didn't want to bed his princess in a field or a wood, as if she were a local trollop, a rough country girl. He asked her to marry him. She said yes. He asked her to tell her parents. She said not yet. He wondered if she were ashamed of him, but was too proud to ask. The letters that travelled between them their last winter apart, with the compliant Norwich Road cousin still acting as postman, were occasionally bitter on his part, reproaching her with not loving as he did (was it possible she had another lover in Edinburgh?) and sad and angry on hers, to be followed, of course, by his abject apologies, his hurt and pain.

That year she was ten days late at her cousin's: her mother had been ill and she couldn't leave home until the third week in July. By the evening, when they met in the churchyard, he was weak with desire. They embraced by the tombstone of Aunt's great-grandfather, James Wilberforce Mudd, who had died in his eightieth year, and lay down on his grave. Effie whispered, 'Give me a baby.'

Afterwards, he was appalled. She had cried out when he entered her. He saw she was bleeding. He cleaned her up with tufts of

54

damp churchyard grass and dried her with the clean linen handkerchief Aunt had told him a 'gentleman' must always carry. He thought it unlikely that Aunt had envisaged this use for it.

He said, 'Are you all right, my love?' and although moonlit tears shone on the end of her lashes, she smiled at him so sweetly he thought his heart would break.

He lowered his voice respectfully. 'Where are your underclothes? You'll get cold,' and she laughed.

'I came out without any knickers, you booby. I thought we'd never get around to it otherwise.'

He pulled her up to her feet and held her at arm's length. She was wearing a long-waisted shift of green silk that reached to her knees and a necklace of crystal beads that sparkled like her tears. He said, 'Lucky those didn't get broken.'

'I'll take them off next time.'

'*Next time*,' he said gruffly, 'we'll be married.'

He was in Edinburgh four days later. He had sent a letter to the Writer to the Signet, saying he would be in the city that day and would be happy to see him at whatever time was convenient. He stated his business as personal and referred Effie's father to the letter she had written to her mother by the same post.

The Writer to the Signet said, 'I have read what my daughter wrote to her mother. My wife is prostrated. She has not left her bed since the letter arrived. I must tell you that I hold you entirely responsible. Of course, Effie will return home immediately, and there will be no more correspondence between you. Nor between my daughter and her cousin whose conduct has been most reprehensible, though her husband is more at fault to my mind. Young women are weak in these matters. I blame the reading of novels. That is all I have to say to you, young man. You may think yourself lucky to have got off so lightly.'

His tone hinted at unbelievable horrors in store for anyone who dared to defy him. Silas wondered what exactly he had in mind. And, anxiously, if there was anything he could in fact do. He said, 'Effie loves me. We have loved each other for five years. I would have declared myself before if Effie had been willing. Perhaps she wanted to spare you until she was absolutely sure. Or wait until I was able to support her, which I am now, sir, I can assure you. I have my accounts with me, should you wish to see them, and a letter from my bank.'

Effie's father waved a long, thin, white hand dismissively, 'I have no wish to see any credentials. You are quite unsuitable for my daughter in every way. There is nothing more to be said.'

He stood behind his desk. He was formidably tall and very old; an old, hawk's face; eyes sharp and gleaming in their wrinkled sockets.

Silas said, 'It's too late, sir.' He hesitated. How to make it clear? This was his only chance. He said, 'She is already mine. I have taken her maidenhead. She could be pregnant. And she is twenty-one next week.'

Later, he was amazed at himself. He was momentarily afraid; the blood sang in his ears. Then the old hawk sat—or rather crumpled—in his chair. He put his head in his hands and Silas knew he had beaten him. Aunt was right. *Always come out straight with what you mean, don't shilly-shally, that's the way to lose the argument.* He said, 'I'm sorry, sir. But I do love her. We do love each other.'

*　　*　　*

The old man never got used to it, but he endured it with an adequate grace as Silas, much, much later, understanding more, endured his daughters' marriages to men he disliked or despised. He despised Alice's now vanished husband because he was a rogue and an absconder. Although he had always been uneasy with Hannah's professor because they seemed to have so little to say to each other, he could see that Julius was a kind, clever man, the best husband he could have imagined for his blustery, opinionated, difficult daughter. It was only in the last ten years that he had grown to dislike Julius for what was beginning to seem a condescending attitude to himself; as if now Silas was old and deaf, Julius considered himself so much Silas's intellectual superior that he would never bother to argue a point with him. It was always *yes, sir, no sir, three bags full, sir,* and always with that gently compassionate smile.

It seems to Silas now, that Julius treats him like an old man to be pandered to, pitied. Hannah has caught the habit. (Unless Julius caught it from her.) *Yes, Father, no, Father. Would you like to lie down for a little while, Father?*

Alice—well, for a while after Bella died, he had found Alice good company. He had even stayed with her once, a rare visit to her cottage on the lake in Maine, and she had talked to him about her work, how important the laboratory mice were for her research, being so swiftly productive, so many generations in so few weeks, how similar to humans genetically, how the different diets they were given added to our understanding of the difference between nature and nurture. Sitting on her deck in the early morning, idly watching the loons and the cormorants, a pair of red squirrels chasing round a tree trunk and, as the sun got up, the pretty blue damsel flies, he wondered if he had taken in what she told him.

Later, swimming in the cold lake, his skinny old body white in the clear, brown water, he decided that her work remained mysterious to him. But he had felt at peace with her all the same, with this clever daughter who didn't patronise him or seem to be worried about him.

Halcyon days—and short-lived. The appalling children telephoned, asking Alice for money presumably, and sent 'love to Gramps'. Silas kept his mouth shut about the children. But then, without warning, the lover returned. He was younger than Alice's own eldest son but much the same in appearance, filthy hair in dreadlocks, mooching about in a pair of dirty pink undershorts, cigarette dangling from loose-lipped, amiable mouth. Silas said to Alice, 'How can you bear it?'

And left, the next day. He tried, later, to speak to Will. 'Your sister. She's taken up with this man, well, not a man, more a hobbledehoy . . .'

Will had said, gravely, 'Hobbledehoy, hobbledehoy, neither a man not yet a boy', that's what you mean, isn't it? Oh, I don't know, Father.'

'Sex,' Silas had said. 'Only sex. And she didn't care if I heard them at it. Thin walls, you know. She was brought up decently, Will. She should look a bit higher.'

'She's a grown woman, Father. She has made her own choices.'

Priggish, Silas had thought. Pompous young ass!

A year or two after that, Will turned fifty. The same age as the Writer to the Signet had been when Silas had asked him for his daughter's hand. The same age as the old hawk, crumpling into defeat behind his desk. But Will wasn't old, Silas tells himself with amazement. He is *his youngest child.* With a weak chest. *No stamina.*

'He won't make old bones,' he had said to Coral. Regretted it afterwards, she might take it amiss. He had only meant she should look after him better. He supposes she thinks her career is important. Certainly Molly had thought so. But what, in the end, did it amount to? A pile of bones, a heap of dust, only living in the minds of those who had loved and survived you. Who would remember Molly once he had gone? Or him, for that matter? Or Will or Coral?

CHAPTER FIVE

Coral kisses Will. they press hands and smile at each other with guarded affection. He says, 'Good luck. Take care, darling.'

She says, 'You, too!'

It is late now. The visiting hours for the main wards are long over. Side wards, reserved for patients who are either dying, or whose condition is temporarily serious, are allowed friends and family at any time, within the discretion of the medical staff and the ward sister. Visitors leaving at this late hour could be seen either as privileged or as unfortunate. They glance at each other as they assemble outside the lift, making covert assessments. Coral thinks it unlikely, from his calm, unmoved expression, that the man in the beautiful green cap has been sitting by a deathbed. As they enter the lift together, she smiles experimentally.

He responds with a nod, a tentative grin, and a hunching of the shoulders and a—slightly Italian—spreading of the fingers, starfishing his hand as if to say, Who's to know?

There are three others with them, two men and a grey, weary-looking, middle-aged woman—one of the corpsewatchers, Coral surmises. When they reached the ground floor, the woman whispers to Coral, 'Do you know where the toilet is?'

Coral gestures towards the silhouette of a pin-person with a skirt. And says, 'Not a bad idea, either.'

She hears the woman weeping in the next stall and decides that she is in no mood to act as comfort or counsellor. Her own eyes are wet and there is an ache in her throat. She leaves before the woman emerges and hurries through the glass doors of the hospital entrance.

The snow is blowing in the wind; icy pats of hail sting her cheeks. A car draws up at the bottom of the steps and the passenger door is pushed open. The velvet cap lies on the passenger seat. The owner picks it up and throws it in the back. He says, 'Can I give you a lift? Beastly night.'

She comes down the steps. He says, 'Smoking. Did you guess that was his trouble? Constriction of the arteries. Both legs amputated. Do you smoke?'

He has what she thinks of as an educated Midland accent; almost received pronunciation, but with a slight roughness Coral finds attractive.

'I did once. Long ago now. Years! I was at RADA. People smoke in the theatre. But no thank you, I can easily pick up a taxi. I don't live so far. Just a mile north of St Paul's.'

'On my way,' he says. 'Absolutely no trouble.'

Silly to refuse. Ridiculous. What is she afraid of? Will would laugh at her! What possible reason . . .?

She says, 'That's very kind. If you would drop me at the Angel, Islington, it would be wonderful. If you're sure it's not out of your way.'

He shakes his head. Laughs. As she slides into the passenger seat she sees he is younger than she is but not all that much younger. His mouth is lined, the flesh stretched under his chin. Did that make him more, or less, dangerous? Why should she think of danger?

He leans across her and closes the door. His arm brushes her breast as he reaches for her seat-belt. 'There,' he says, buckling it tight across her. He touches something on his driver's door and there is a hollow thunk.

'There,' he repeats. 'Central locking. Now you are safe from all harm.'

CHAPTER SIX

Dear Popsicle,

Thank you so much for that delicious lunch, it's always fun to be with you and I always come away invigorated and wondering if I should do so much legal aid work! After I've left you I am always inclined to be brisker with some of my sad clients than perhaps I ought to be! It's not really their fault that they're not endowed with your energy and panache but it's not all in the genes either! Davey agrees with me that we have both learned from you that character and will are equally important. When I say 'learned' I don't mean that you have ever preached, it is your example that has taught us . . .

That's enough of that! I wouldn't want

to give you a swelled head! It is just that sometimes when I've had a happy hour or so with you, I long to tell you what a wonderful LIFE FORCE you are, what a wonderful EXEMPLAR!

I only wish Mummy could be here to help us celebrate your birthday as I expect you do, too! I am sure it will be a splendid occasion and I am so touched and flattered that you want me to sit close to you and be your interpreter!

Thank you for showing me how to live!

Very much love from your loving,

Clare

When he has read this letter, Will returns it to Silas, sitting beside his hospital bed in the main ward to which he has been moved early this morning. Will keeps his face stiff. 'Very nice, Father. Nice appreciative girl.'

Silas nods and folds the letter slowly and very neatly before returning it to his small, worn, brown leather wallet, which he then closes with an old elastic band, twisted round twice to make it secure. He puts away the wallet in an inner pocket of his jacket, pats the pocket, adjusts his lapels, and says, 'I've had photocopies made. I sent one to Alice and one to Hannah.'

Will says, 'Ah,' and looks thoughtful.

Silas says, 'I thought, perhaps Deborah?'

'Dinkie? Oh, I don't know. You know what

they're like at that age.' He smiles, coaxing Silas to share his fatherly amusement while trying, at the same time, to dismiss from his mind the image of his fourteen-year old daughter's disgusted face and the theatrical imitation of vomiting, which would be her reaction to this flowery tribute to her grandfather. He says, 'I'm not sure, Father. I mean that's a private letter. Don't you think Clare might be upset if you showed it around?'

Silas looks uncomprehending. Perhaps he hasn't heard. He is playing with his ancient hearing-aid, turning it up until it squeals.

Will wants to say, 'She only wrote it to please you.' But then that seems cruel to Silas. He, Will, had been cruel to Coral last night when she came to see him. At least he had thought, by her expression when she left, that he had somehow upset her. She had annoyed him, too, though he couldn't quite recall how or why at the moment. If she had been a bit dense, or silly, which was usually the sort of thing that made him irritable with her, she had every excuse. She had been exhausted, poor girl. Who wouldn't be after dining with an about-to-be centenarian followed by a duty hospital visit to an invalid husband? Not for the first time this winter, either! He'd had his prostate fixed two months ago, late November, humiliating operation. Or he had felt humiliated, anyway. He had (wrongly, it turned out) doubted his cheerful surgeon's robust assurances and convinced himself that impotence was the most likely result of this disagreeable exercise. He had felt, during what Coral with an ominous (though presumably unintended) resonance had referred to as his *lying in*, as if a huge placard hung over his bed, visible (though of course never mentioned) to each and every visitor. EMASCULATED. UNMANNED.

He had felt this most keenly when Silas came to see him, flying in from Menton where he often spent the late autumn after the crowds had left and hotels were cheaper and before the 'geriatrics'—Silas's term even for people in their seventies, thirty years younger than he was—settled along the length of that coast for the winter. There was little chance that Silas, whose interest in any human condition other than perfectly operating health was minimal, had any idea that prostate operations could sometimes cause impotence. All the same, Will had suffered torments of inadequacy while Silas sat beside his bed. It was as if he had been reduced by his father's presence to an artificial childhood, reliving moments when he had fallen and hurt himself, or been discovered in tears for an even more shameful reason, a looming dentist's appointment or a broken toy, and been told to grow up, *to be a man*.

Looked at from that angle, pneumonia is a less embarrassing illness, he tells himself, and finds himself grinning absurdly. It seems to him that Silas is looking puzzled. Well, no wonder. Ninety-nine years old, sitting by the sickbed of his weakling son, half his age, for the second time this winter, what has the boy got to laugh about? He says, hastily, 'How old is Clare, Father?'

'Thirty-nine.'

This answer comes surprisingly pat. Had Silas taken over Bella's diary, or perhaps a birthday book, when she died? Sent cards and cheques to Bella's children as well as his own? Well, why not?

Silas says, 'Clare was just nineteen when I married Bella.' He takes a handkerchief from his trouser pocket and wipes his eyes and his nose.

Will opens a creaky door in his mind and enters the registrar's office in Rosebery Avenue, Finsbury, on a chilly June day twenty years ago. Coral was wearing the yellow dress she had worn for their wedding and she had cried when she put it on because the waist was unexpectedly tight. Hannah and Julius had been there but not Alice who was in Australia, giving an important lecture in Sydney. Or it might have been Melbourne or Canberra. (It is difficult to keep up with Alice's international appearances.) Her second son had come in her place and had worn a suit of pale grey silk but this imaginative effort to please his grandfather had been somewhat negated by a metal safety-pin attached to his left eyebrow. Bella's son, on the other hand, Davey the doctor, had turned up looking noble and young and exhausted after a night on call, soberly dressed and wearing a tie.

Clare had appeared older then, Will remembers. Of course, girls of nineteen could sometimes seem matronly. He says, 'I think I thought she must have been at least in her twenties. Old enough to be on her own, self-supporting. Or she would have been living with Bella. Well, living with you and Bella . . .'

Even as he speaks, he knows this is an absurd suggestion. Silas is laughing and shaking his head. 'Hardly likely to set up house again, was I? Past that stage. Clare was at university. Vacations, she usually went to her aunt in Athens. Or stayed with Davey. Nice girl, tactful, affectionate. Well, you see what I mean with that letter.'

'Yes.'

'But you think I shouldn't have sent it to Alice and Hannah.'

Will sighs. 'I don't know, Father. All I can say is, I don't think I would have done. Which isn't to say you were wrong. Just that I wouldn't have done it.'

His father makes the harrumphing sound with which he normally signals disagreement bordering on contempt for someone else's arguments. Fair enough in this case, Will considers. His contribution has been quite

68

startlingly inept. He says, speaking slowly, hoping to convey the impression that after a period of really serious thought he is now presenting a considered judgement, 'I think they may be hurt. Very hurt indeed. I mean, it isn't their style, neither Hannah's nor Alice's, and they may think if that is the sort of thing you like, the sort of thing that pleases you, then they must have let you down badly. Just because they express themselves differently, in a more reserved manner than Clare, doesn't mean they are not just as affectionate.'

He sees the old man thinks this is a load of cobblers. Well, it is, isn't it? Neither of his sisters is likely to respond quite like that. Oh, be honest! He might not care for them all that much but neither of them is remotely capable of that sort of bilge. Alice would most likely laugh and dismiss it; she has more interesting things to take up her time. She might, if she was in that sort of mood, call young Clare something like 'a cunning little vixen' but without any real malice. Hannah is another matter. He could just see her at the breakfast table, tossing the letter over to poor Julius, innocently eating his toast and drinking his coffee. Before he had a chance to read it, Hannah would be red in the face and gobbling. *You can see what she's after. Always has been, she and her mother. You'd think she'd screwed enough out of him . . .*

Thank Christ he is out of the way, safe in

hospital. The only telephone available is of the kind that has to be wheeled to your bed by a busy nurse if you can't get up and if you are ambulant (as Will is now, has been since this morning) searched for throughout this enormous public ward that consists of a ribbon development of nurses' stations, showers, lavatories, and treatment rooms with ten small six-bedded wards leading off. Even if you could track down the telephone it is usually either in use by, or in the close custody of, one of the women's sections. And in Will's recent experience with his prostate (a different hospital, but the same fashionable arrangement of mixed-sex wards) female patients were liable to glare with a terrifying mix of suspicion and spite at any male who approached the telephone trolley. In these circumstances the likelihood of Hannah being able to seek and destroy him is remote.

Silas says, 'I don't believe I was trying to put them in the wrong. I thought they would like to see that loving little letter. Clare is a clever girl, she's got a good mind, but she has a kind and simple heart. Show it to Coral, see what she thinks. Have you spoken to her this morning? I was a bit surprised, she usually rings me at the Club before breakfast. To ask if I've had a good night, see if I want anything.' He adds, in what Will hears as a grudging tone, 'Very good of her.'

'She was going off early, down to Brighton. I

meant to ring her, but I didn't have time. They moved me out of that side ward the moment I woke, around six o'clock, all in a rush. An emergency coming in, I suppose, though no one seemed to know. You know what it's like in hospitals . . .'

He reflects that this is one thing about which Silas is almost totally ignorant. His only spell in hospital (in Athens, with the same lung infection that had killed Bella) had been too brief to acquaint him with the normally anarchic nature of hospital life. He is looking around him now with a furtively puzzled air as if he found the scene not just strange, but uniquely and grotesquely alarming. The amputee in the bed opposite Will has pushed off his bedclothes so that a great flange of mottled purplish flesh is exposed, a thick stump of thigh ending in a puckered scar that looks like a blind, searching, underground creature as it shifts from side to side, gently and slowly, apparently quite independent of the patient to whom it belongs who is wired up to a drip and a tangle of breathing apparatus and reading the *Daily Telegraph*. In the next bed to the amputee, a skeletal head, yellow skin stretched tight over jutting bone, lies motionless on the pillows, and on his other side, a young Somali sits cross-legged on top of his bedclothes, wearing green hospital pyjamas and nervously rolling the whites of his eyes. These three fellow patients are already familiar to Will who is accustomed to making hospital friends quickly and easily. He is on first-name terms with the Somali and the skull-head, with Ahmed and with John; the amputee is a much older man who has introduced himself as Mr Thornley with a firm emphasis on the Mr. Will's bed, which faces these three, is effectively screened from his side of the ward by the one next to him, which has been curtained off ever since his arrival. Its occupant has been coughing spasmodically, dreadful, tearing and retching coughs that make Silas frown.

After a particularly violent bout, Silas says, 'You ought to be in a private room. This isn't healthy.'

He speaks in a deaf man's loud voice and from behind the curtain comes a desperate, gasping hiccup of laughter. Will says, equally loudly, 'It's a good chest hospital, Father. I don't think they have private rooms. My insurance has run out, anyway.'

Silas is fiddling with his hearing-aid again. To avoid any embarrassing discussion about money? Unwilling to offer to pay his invalid son's medical bills? No doubt that's what Coral would say!

Silas says, 'If Coral's going to be working next week, would you like Clare to pay you a visit? If you're likely to be stuck here much longer. She had lunch with me the other day, Thursday I think, and suggested it. She said

72

she's always wanted to get to know you and Coral better.'

'Nothing to stop her,' Will says. Should he point out that they had lived in the same city for quite a few years? Before Bella died, she and Silas had occasionally given a family dinner party when they were staying in London, inviting Clare along with Coral and Will, but although Will thinks he can pin down a couple of chance meetings since Bella's death—a theatre foyer comes to mind, an exhibition at the Hayward Gallery—he is sure there had never been any arranged social occasion. He knows he has never seen Clare's apartment and has no memory of her in his house in Islington.

'Bella had hoped you might take an interest in Clare when she started working in London,' Silas says. This time the reproach is evident.

'If she'd wanted to see us we would have been glad to see her. She had only to ring, get in touch. But she didn't.'

'Coral is the older woman. You were the married couple. It was up to you to invite her.'

'I suppose we never thought of it like that,' Will says, in a peaceably reflective voice. 'She was much younger, we were busy working and having babies. We would have assumed she had better things to do with her time.'

Silas is frowning. 'The poor girl's an orphan.'

'We all become orphans some time or

73

another.'

This might not turn out to be true of himself, Will reflects. Has Father thought of that? What would it be like for him not just to lose a child through illness or accident but to *outlive* him through a combination of indomitable genes and a saving self-regard? He says, 'Of course I would be delighted to see Clare any time, Father, though I think I'll be out of this place very soon now. But just as soon as I'm sprung, and Coral's finished with *Hamlet*, and I've caught up at the office, I promise you, we'll ask her round for an evening. Family party, we'll see if Rory and Pippa can get down to London. Not always easy to get away from colleges in term time, but I'm sure they'd be pleased to know Clare a bit better. What is the relationship? Aunt-by-marriage?'

Silas is looking discomfited as Will had expected. An innocent heartiness is the best way to damp down the sudden flurries of indignation that afflict his father, flaring up in small, explosive puffs—like marsh gas, Will thinks, uncertain why this image should come into his mind. The fen of an old man's digestion belching forth foulness? Though Silas has no intestinal problems, indeed no real medical problems at all except deafness and the gathering weakness of age. Oh, he would naturally resent that, any diminution of physical power, but he would be more

74

affronted by his inability to control other people's behaviour—*go there, do that, believe what I tell you*—as he had once been able to do.

'Step-sister,' Silas says. 'Clare is their step-aunt, your step-sister. Same generation. A few years between you. Rather more between Clare and your sisters, of course. But don't trouble yourself. As you say by now the girl's got her own life. What might have been welcome once, may be redundant now. Just an embarrassment to her.'

Will says, under his breath, 'Okay, you win.'

'Whassay? I'm not picking you up. Never mind. Time I went, I dare say. Always feel sorry for patients in hospital, can't escape from their visitors. Besides, cab's got the meter ticking up, got him to wait, couldn't just trust to luck finding one, my age, this weather.'

He reaches for his sticks and begins the slow process of getting to his feet, frowning with concentration, encouraging himself with little grunts of effort.

Will finds this performance painful to watch. He says, 'I'll see you to the lift.'

He knows why Silas shakes his head. He dislikes anyone seeing the effort it costs him to move his body around. All the same, Will says, 'It'll do me good, a bit of a walk.' And although he had been taller than his father for a long time, he is shocked to see how small and bent the old man is now as he hobbles crabwise beside him.

A man has already called the lift and, seeing Silas approaching, holds it for him. Will smiles his thanks; Silas nods and draws himself up proudly. The man has one wrist in a sling, his expensive-looking coat shrugged over that shoulder, and he is wearing a velvet corduroy cap, the kind of headgear that Will can hear Silas calling a nancy-boy's titfer. Will prays that Silas will not say this aloud; mercifully, his father's eye falls on the man's wounded arm and he says, as he enters the lift, 'You been in trouble?'

The man says something Will doesn't hear, and the doors close behind them.

*   *   *

'Nothing,' the man says. 'Nothing to bring me to a hospital, anyway. I've been to see my mother.' He gave a sharp laugh. 'In a manner of speaking, that is. I've been watching her die.'

They have reached the ground floor. The lift doors open. The man says, 'In the cancer ward. She had lung cancer. She never smoked in her life.'

It seems to Silas that this total stranger is alarmingly close to tears. And he is alone in the lift with him. He says, hastily, shrinking from this intolerable display of emotion, 'At least you're fully grown. My mother died when

76

I was four years old.'

They have reached the ground floor. The doors open. Silas said, 'I'm sorry for your loss,' but the man has gone, his full skirts swirling behind him.

CHAPTER SEVEN

Silas was four years old. This was before Swaffham, before Aunt. Molly was at school. May, the new baby, was fussing in her crib under the window, letting out small squeaks and damp, mumbling sounds. He stood in the doorway of his parents' bedroom looking at his mother, who was sitting at her dressing-table in her night clothes, looking at herself in the mirror, and weeping. She hadn't got properly dressed this morning, nor for several mornings now. She rocked from side to side on the dressing-stool, turning her face from the mirror and cradling it in her hands. She looked sad, but pretty. Silas thought she was beautiful, even when she was sad. He didn't know why she was crying and he loved her so much, it gave him a pain in his chest.

She said, 'Siley, oh, Siley, I can't bear it any longer, I'm so dreadfully ill, I'm no use, no use at all, I can't even look after Baby. She cries so much and it hurts my poor head.'

They were living in the house in London

where they had all been born. Their father had lost his job and they had no money so they had let the ground-floor front room to Mr and Mrs Bright. Mr Bright was out in the day but Mrs Bright was always at home because she had a bad leg and sometimes she looked after Baby May. Silas said, 'Don't cry, Mummy, please don't cry, I'll take May down to Mrs Bright, then I'll make you a nice cup of tea.'

He lifted the wet, grizzling baby out of her cradle and carried her down the stairs, stepping carefully, because the brown linoleum on the treads was worn and slippy. When he reached Mrs Bright's door, he couldn't knock because he needed both arms to hold May, but Mrs Bright heard her crying and opened the door and took her from him just as he began to feel he couldn't hold her much longer. Mrs Bright said, 'There, there, Baby May, come to Brighty!' And to Silas, 'Mummy not so well this morning? Thought I could hear her. Never you mind, though, she's not the first poor woman to get the downs after a baby.' And she cuddled May close to her fat chest until the baby started to nuzzle the front of her blouse. Mrs Bright laughed and said, 'Sorry, young lady, Brighty can't oblige in that department but you be a good girl and we'll find you some sugar water.'

The room smelt horrible. Before Mr and Mrs Bright came, it had always smelt fresh and nice. Mummy had opened the window each

78

morning, and kept the fireplace shiny and black and the round walnut table smelling of cedar polish. The room was always clean and tidy because they hardly ever used it except at Christmas, or on Sundays, or when visitors came. Now it was untidy as well as smelly. Mr Bright's underwear, once white, now yellow, was hanging on the guard in front of the fire, the jangly brass bed (at least it was jangly when Mr and Mrs Bright both got into it when the noise sang through the house) was unmade, and the chamber-pot under the bed was still full from the night. Mrs Bright patted Baby May's bottom and put her down on the grubby bed, saying, 'That's the first job, my lady, meantime, if your big brother fancies a biscuit he might just find one in the red tin.'

The red tin was kept in the right-hand cupboard of the sideboard along with Mr Bright's whisky. The biscuits were a bit dry but Silas was hungry. He was hungry a lot of the time nowadays. He ate several of the dry biscuits, an apple from the fruit bowl, and then drank a cup of milk that Mrs Bright waddled out of the room to fetch from the jug on the shelf in the kitchen larder where she kept her provisions, renting this shelf along with the room and the use of the wash-house. While he ate, he watched her clean up Baby May's bottom and give her a drink of sugar water from a bottle, and rock her to sleep.

When he finally, reluctantly, went back

upstairs, his mother was dead.

She was lying on the floor by the side of the bed, her lovely hair loose and spread all around her. She lay on her stomach with one arm stretched out and her head turned so that he could see her open mouth with a trail of slimy stuff coming out of it, and one glazed, open eye. He knew she was dead at once but all the same he said, 'Mummy, Mummy, wake up,' and knelt beside her, not daring to touch her. When, after quite a long while, he saw there was dust in her open eye, he knew he should go down and call Mrs Bright, but he didn't want her to see his mother lying helpless like this. His mother had said Mrs Bright was a good soul but 'common', and although he wasn't quite sure what 'common' meant, he knew that his mother would be upset if Mrs Bright found her dead on the floor. His mother would rather be found dead on her bed. It would be more respectable.

She was amazingly heavy. She had always looked so delicate and thin beside Silas's father when he swung her up in his arms, high above his head, as he sometimes did to Silas. Baby May was still too small for that kind of junketing, and Molly too big now, but their mother was light as a pretty bird's feather. That was what their father always said. Not now, however, not for Silas; she was not only heavier beyond anything he had ever lifted, but she was limp and soggy. He thought—like a sack of wet coal dust. He had once, when the rain had got in through a cracked pavement cover, helped his father clean out the coal cellar. But she wasn't a sack of coal. She was his mother. And struggling with her, he had to get hold of private parts of her body, so that he was both ashamed, and afraid in case she woke up and caught him with his fingers where they shouldn't be.

It was over an hour of sobbing and gasping before he managed to heave her, first on the long footstool, then, twisting her round and pulling and pushing, right up on to the bed. He knew how long it had taken him because he watched the time tick by, and heard the hour strike, in the carriage clock on the mantelpiece that Aunt Geneva, their father's sister, had given to her brother when he got married. Engraved round the face were the words *Let Time Be Your Servant, Never Your Master.* When Silas had finally arranged his mother quite tidily, her head on a pillow, her legs covered with her cotton wrapper, he sat beside her for what seemed like a hundred years, keeping as still as she was. He screwed up his eyes and whispered under his breath, 'If I keep my eyes shut and count backwards like Molly says, when I open them she'll be standing there, all alive, in the corner.'

But when he opened his eyes, she hadn't moved, there was a trail of something pale and horrid that had run out of her mouth and

81

dried on her skin, and her hands were cold.

When Molly came home from school, she found Silas curled up on the floor in the exact place where their mother had fallen earlier, his clenched fists pressed tight against his eyes.

*   *   *

He had never been told what had killed her. All that had stayed with him from that dreadful day was the noise his father had made when he came home later on, throwing himself on the bed beside his dead wife and weeping. Brighty had fetched them away and closed the door of her room but the noise still came through the ceiling, a hollow, menacing, groaning sound like the boom of fog-horns on the river. Brighty held Baby May on her lap and sat Molly and Silas at the table and made them sing hymns. 'There is a green hill far away, Without a city wall.' She said, 'You must all try to be glad that your dear mother is at peace now, safe in heaven in the kind arms of Jesus.'

Then Aunt was there, with her red cheeks and her rough hands, and her high, loud voice, filling the little house with her bustle and energy that was frightening and comforting at the same time. The tin bath in the kitchen was filled with hot water and he and Molly had to get in stark naked, both together, and Aunt scrubbed them until they were red and tingling all over. 'Cleaner than you've ever been,' she said, in a grumbling voice as she used a twist of towel to poke into Silas's ears as a final touch. Then she gave them new clothes to put on that were not quite the right size: the trousers and jacket she had bought for Silas were tight round his chest and his middle and Molly's were loose all over except for the stiff Eton collar she was made to put on, which pinched her neck and scratched the soft flesh under her chin. She grumbled to their father who said, almost whispering as if he was afraid Aunt would hear, 'Don't make a fuss, my dearest girl, it's very good of Geneva, she wants you to look nice for the funeral.'

*　　*　　*

All he remembered from his mother's funeral was the feel of Aunt's hard, consoling hand holding his, and the fusty geranium smell of her best black coat as he buried his face in it. At Baby May's funeral, Aunt wore the same coat, shinier now, and so tight at the seams that it showed the stitches, but he was too big a boy to have his hand held and he had to walk alone behind his sister's small coffin as the Vicar went ahead, clanging a bell and intoning, 'I am the resurrection and the life.' 'Your father can't be here so you are the man of the family and have to go first,' Aunt had said. 'Just hold your head up and look straight

83

ahead till you get to the front pew. Molly and I will be right behind you.'

He had a pain low down in his stomach and he was afraid he would dirty himself. Although he had done his business that morning (and before they left the house, Aunt had sent him out again, to make sure) fear of this terrible shame occupied him all through the service. Even when they were in the graveyard at last and Aunt told him to throw earth on the coffin, all he could think of was that it was nearly over now and he would soon be back in the house. The outside privy might be cold and full of spiders, a place to be avoided until the very last moment, but just now it was safety and home. Molly saw the screwed-up fear in his face and whispered, 'Don't be scared, just squeeze your bottom tight and nothing will happen. Molly's here, she'll take care of you.'

Molly had been crying, slimy tracks of tears down her cheeks, and her eyes were red. It made her look ugly. He knew she had loved their little sister and it made him uncomfortable. He wished he felt as she did so that he could be sad with her, because he loved Molly, but he wasn't sorry Baby May was dead. It was her fault that his mother had died. Before she was born his mother had been happy. She had spent most of the day with him, singing to him and reading to him out of *Books For The Bairns*. And when his father was home they were always laughing together.

Baby May had made her too ill to play with him or laugh with his father. If Baby May was going to die she should have died earlier, while his mother was still alive. Then his mother might have got better.

He thought that he hated Baby May now, for dying at the wrong time.

He knew that he mustn't say this to Molly because it would hurt her. He could have said it to Aunt, though he didn't understand that until many years later, a married man and a father, watching three-year old Hannah, screaming with outrage over some small frustration or other, and remembering, suddenly, his aunt Geneva coming down the stairs of the cottage in Swaffham dressed for Baby May's funeral in her shiny black coat, redder in the face than usual and trumpeting into her handkerchief. She had said, 'Oh, she was a real little devil, the Lord knows, but I'm going to miss her.' And then, to Silas, with one of her angry sniffs, 'More than you will, I dare say, and I can't say I blame you, poor little cocker, put your nose out of joint, so a little bird told me.'

And then, quite unexpectedly, she swept Silas up in her arms and sat in the rocker and held him fiercely to her flat chest while she sent the old chair creaking backwards and forwards so wildly that he was sure they would both be sent flying and crack their heads open on the stone flags of the floor, something Aunt had often warned him about if he sat in the rocker. He was relieved all the same: the violence of Aunt's embrace meant that she had forgiven him.

Not that she had ever blamed him, he realised afterwards. Not even in the first dreadful moment when she came from the kitchen and saw the child tipped over the edge of the old water butt, held there by her sash that had caught on a nail, short fat legs in white frilly drawers sticking up straight and still, and Silas, at the far end of the long narrow garden, back turned to the tragedy, absorbed in his work: a delicate pattern of broken white shells decorating the castle he was drawing in the flinty dust. Aunt had shouted, 'Silas, go into the summerhouse and don't come out till I come for you. Quick sharp. Now. Go. This minute.'

He had looked up, bewildered, to see her standing at the back door, holding her skirts spread like wings. She was hiding the water butt from him, he knew that, and perhaps he had even known why, but it was not until all those years later, holding his daughter Hannah stiff with anger in his arms, that he allowed himself to acknowledge that he might just have seen his wilful little sister drag the three-legged stool to the side of the butt, the stool he had told her half a dozen times to leave alone, not to touch . . .

And had turned his back.

CHAPTER EIGHT

Hannah, just out of bed, robed in a voluminous dressing-gown (pink polyester sprinkled with daisies that has been purchased, as all her clothes are, by mail order), billows majestically into the warm kitchen of her house in Yorkshire, waving a sheet of paper in her right hand. With her left, she slaps a bundle of mail in front of her husband, Julius, who is dressed in a stiff Guernsey sweater, jeans, thick socks and a knitted hat and is eating porridge richly slathered with thick cream and brown sugar from a blue and white pottery bowl. His muddy outdoor boots stand drying in front of the Aga. He has been out with the flock, letting out the pregnant ewes from the lambing fold where they spend the night, and had hoped to finish his breakfast and read *The Times* in peace before Hannah appeared.

He smiles lovingly at her all the same. He is—perversely or miraculously, depending on the observer—a deeply loving husband, not an uxorious or subservient one. He loves Hannah's moral energy, her apparently endless supply of indignation. Age does not seem to weary her; growing older has in no way diminished her outrage at the wickedness and the folly of the world. This seems remarkable to Julius, who had once burned with such angry grief over his parents (his mother perished in Belsen, his father no one knew where) that he felt he would die of it, but finds it hard nowadays to feel strongly about anything. He also loves Hannah's body, which he knows is unfashionably large but which he finds reassuringly solid and warm. It has consoled him since she was a plump student and he a thin, anxious refugee, astonished and grateful to find peace in her arms. Even now, burrowing into her (especially on the chilly nights of which there are more than he had expected when Hannah first persuaded him to retire to this wild part of Yorkshire), he still feels safe from all harm.

But his protector is vulnerable, too. She is easily hurt, his brave, valiant Hannah.

He says, 'What's he done now? I assume it's your father.'

Smiling, trying to make light in advance of whatever insult is contained in it, he holds out his hand for the letter.

'It's not exactly *from* him. It's a photocopy of a sucking-up hymn of praise that dreadful girl wrote him. Masquerading as a thank-you letter. He seems to have thought I might like to see it. That's what he's scribbled on the top, anyway. *Thought you might like to see this!* Why on earth should he think that? He's sent a copy to Alice, as well. Though of course she won't have got it yet. Not through the post, anyway. I suppose he could have sent it by fax.'

She stands, breathing hard through her nostrils, while Julius reads Clare's letter, taking his time about it, fighting the need to laugh. Though perhaps laughter would be the sensible way to detoxify this piece of nonsense? But Hannah does not laugh easily.

He says, in the end, 'Look, dearest heart. That's a letter from a nice woman who I'd guess was just trying to please a lonely old man. On the other hand, who knows, she might feel what she says. I mean . . .' He pauses, wondering what in fact he does mean, and blunders. 'How old was Clare when her father died? In her early teens, wasn't she? So when Bella married again she may have been eager to make that sort of transference. Looking for another father. Perhaps Silas has always been more important to her than any of us realised.'

' "Life force," ' Hannah says bitterly. ' "Exemplar." '

She drags out a chair, squeaking it horribly on the quarry tiles of the floor, and throws herself into it, slumping crossly, elbows on the table, chin on one hand. Julius pours coffee for her and gets up to make toast on the Aga, lightly stroking the back of her neck as he passes behind her. She shrugs him off impatiently.

'Didn't you *read* it, Jules? She's to sit next to him! So she can pass on what *his own children* are saying! A girl more or less the same age as his granddaughter, our daughter, who's not been invited, not even to sit below the salt! Oh, just as well, I *know* that, so don't tell me . . .' She holds up her hand, imperious as a traffic policeman. 'Unmarried, pregnant, unemployed —why on earth did she have to give up that perfectly good job? She could have taken maternity leave if she wanted a baby so badly, we'd all have turned to and helped however we felt, she ought to have known that. Oh, I suppose it's best Father doesn't set eyes on her in the circumstances. But you'd think Clare would have more sense than to boast about her sneaky triumph, getting the old man's ear as well as his money, pride of place at his party, sweeping his own children aside! Well, not sense, exactly. Sensibility, I mean. Plain ordinary tact.'

'I wouldn't have said she was boasting, exactly . . .' As soon as he has spoken Julius knows this was unwise.

Hannah says, 'Oh, I might have known you'd stick up for her! Are you claiming he's taught you how to live, too?'

Turning over the browning toast on the Aga, Julius debates with himself. Keeping his mouth shut is often the safest course. Though maybe not in this case. She could interpret his silence as contempt for the anger and pain she was certainly feeling. Or worse, indifference to it.

He says, very gently, 'I'm sorry, darling, I'm not really obtuse. I think I know how you feel. It's not really the seating arrangements. Or the money. Or only partly. It's the tone of the letter.'

Hannah thumps her fist on the table. 'We ought to have a power of attorney.'

Julius cannot help laughing now. Hannah frowns but then smiles, reluctantly. She says, 'Oh, all right, I *know*. He's still got his marbles. But suppose he *goes off*? I mean, *suddenly* . . . Has to have an emergency operation, for example. Anaesthetics *finish* old people quite often.'

'Why don't you tell him that? Present him with this cheerful possibility and ask him what he suggests?'

'Don't be silly.'

Hannah heaps sugar into her coffee and glares, offended, at the far wall of the kitchen.

Julius heaps wholemeal toast on a plate and sits down beside her. He puts his hand over hers. He says, greatly daring, 'Perhaps, all it is, all he's saying, sending that letter around, is "Look, here's someone who seems to feel something for me. Admire me." A way of asking "Do you love me?"'

'Oh, God, how pathetic.' Hannah rolls her eyes to the ceiling.

'Yes. Look at it another way. I know you're fond of your father but does he know it, I wonder?'

91

Hannah groans. Then says, waspishly, 'She's not affectionate. Just devious. She reckons the old fool will respond to flattery and fakery so she lays it on as thick as she dares. Mawkish and sentimental. Just like her mother.'

'I thought you liked Bella!'

'Well. I didn't dislike her. Not to begin with. And she took care of him. And he seemed to be happy. But she did all right on it, didn't she? Lived the life of Riley while she lived. I don't suppose you ever realised what she spent on those dreadful clothes, just because they were vulgar didn't mean they came cheap, and fixing it so that when she died that girl and her brother did all right too.'

'I don't think it was quite like that,' Julius murmurs, but she ignores him.

'I never understood why Father allowed himself to be hoodwinked into disinheriting his own children. A big chunk of loot, anyway. And leaving it to Will to tell Alice and me! That was so cowardly! I ought to ring Will, you know. I will *try* after I've had my breakfast, but you know what that hospital's like. I tried to get hold of him yesterday to see how he was, but of course, quite impossible! I said to the receptionist, I said, "The NHS isn't free, you know, we all pay for it out of our taxes, it's not unreasonable that we should expect to be able to find out about our relations when they are sick," but she was very off-hand, better things to do with her time than help me reach my brother was the implication . . . Oh, poor Will. I do hope he'll be all right. He seems to get some sort of trouble every winter just lately. I do worry about him. I know Father does, too. Is there any more of that marmalade? The gingery one?'

Julius gets up from the table and goes to the cupboard. Hannah says, 'Oh, don't bother, darling, there's only salt butter anyway, I couldn't get any unsalted, and you know I can never eat anything sweet with salt butter. If I can't get Will, I'll try Coral again though she was a bit snappy last time. Besides, she's leaving the answerphone on all the time for some reason. Not picking up messages, either. Pip, pip, pip—a whole string of them. Unlike Coral. Oh, I dare say she's got a lot on, Will in the hospital, and she did say she was working this week, but you'd have thought she'd have known I'd be worried.'

Though she sounds reproachful, there is not much zest there any longer, no real indignation. Julius reckons it is safe to make a small joke. He sits beside her and butters a slice of toast for her. He says, 'And, no doubt, you'd thought to read her that letter?'

*　　　*　　　*

Coral hears the telephone ringing, then her own voice on the answerphone. She pulls the feather pillow over her throbbing head and

93

moans to herself, a determined, low croon, until Hannah stops quacking and the mechanical voice announces the time of her call—the wrong time, in fact, because there was a power cut three days ago and no one has adjusted the machine since. This is something that Coral is usually punctilious about, it being important to know if, when, her agent has telephoned, or the theatre, but since she limped home, very late on Saturday night, she has not answered, or made, a single telephone call. She has heard her father-in-law leave a message— 'Coral my dear. Coral? Coral? You're not there? All right then.' A pause for energetic throat-clearing, Silas is determined to conquer his dislike of this modern method of communication. 'Machine, tell your mistress I rang to wish her success in Brighton. Tell her Will was in excellent spirits when I saw him this morning.'

And Dinkie. 'Hi, Mummy, it's me. We're just off to see *Star Wars*. Bit juvenile, you may think, but Ange says we are juveniles, aren't we? Loads of love from us both, love to Dads, tell him get better soon, don't bother to ring back, know you're busy.'

There has been one anonymous call, clicked off as soon as the announcement came on. Nothing from Will—but then he thinks she's in Brighton. There have been several calls from the theatre.

She ought to ring Greg. More than

94

'ought'—it is an imperative. She has never been so remiss about a job in her life. She should have rung him first thing. She could even have said something like, 'I could struggle in, I suppose, if you can't get a replacement. Has anyone ever thought of playing Gertrude as a battered wife?'

But the eye is so puffy she can barely see out of it. And the bruising has spread down her cheek to the side of her mouth. She has been swallowing aspirin and arnica almost hourly without any improvement, but then without these homely medicaments the damage might now be worse.

'Worse' is difficult to imagine, however. Having dragged herself painfully to the bathroom to pee and to splash her face with cold water, she examines her poor face in the magnifying mirror and feels so sickened by the sight that she grows dizzy and has to cling to the basin. The swelling below the eye is monstrous, a soft, pulpy, blue and green sac, bulging and sagging from the lower lid. And the eye itself is awash with blood, a red, bloody pool in which the iris is no longer visible. Mercifully, she can still look out of it; she hopes, grimly, that if she had been unable to see she would have had the sense to make her way to a hospital. Except that the nearest casualty department is in the hospital where Will is recovering from his most recent bout of pneumonia. Certainly that is the hospital to

95

which she would have been taken if she had allowed her kidnapper to call an ambulance.

If he was/is a kidnapper. Is it her doubts about what actually happened that make her so confused and ashamed that she does not want to face Will? Or speak to anyone.

He had driven past the Angel. But that might have been absent-mindedness. Anxiety. He hadn't said who he was visiting in the hospital. If it was someone who was seriously ill he would naturally have been preoccupied. Thinking about his wife—or his partner. Was he gay? You would think she would know at once, working in the theatre, but sometimes her own sexual response affects her judgement. She had been stirred by this man, something about him, his voice, his appearance, his smell—which was maybe just the smell of the car, an expensive, clean, polished-leather smell. And Will had been so unkind. So *unfair*. She had done all she could. She had dined with his father. It would have been sensible, this bitter night, to have gone straight home from the club. Instead, she had gone to the hospital full of loving intentions and left on the edge of tears . . .

She laughs aloud, sharply. So it's all Will's fault, is it, that she had been so ready to get into another man's car? How daft could you get? She had been so cold when she came out of the sheltered warmth of the hospital, she would have accepted a lift from Vlad the

Impaler . . .

And she had not been alarmed to begin with. Once past the Angel, she had said, 'I'm afraid you've overshot my turning. Doesn't matter. Just drop me anywhere here.'

He hadn't answered or looked at her. He was muttering silently—she could see his lips moving but he was making no sound. She said, 'It's all right, I can get out at the next light. There isn't much traffic.'

She unfastened her seat-belt. He stopped the car as the light turned red. She said, reaching for the door handle, 'Thank you so much for the lift, I really *am* grateful.'

But the door was locked.

Even then she had only been irritated. 'Oh dear, I forgot. Central locking,' she said, with a little trill of laughter to conceal her annoyance. Because, of course, it was too late now, the light had turned amber.

It was then she had realised that he wasn't listening, had not, perhaps, at any point heard her, and felt the first stir of fear. She lifted her voice to (almost) full volume. 'Stop the car, please. I want to get out.'

He didn't look at her. He was muttering again, this time audibly, though she could only barely make out what he said. '. . . to talk to . . . just talk . . . not much to ask, is it?'

He was driving fast now, up the main road. He went through a red traffic light and swerved round a corner, tyres screaming.

Coral said, forcing herself to breathe steadily, deeply, 'Look, if we could stop, we could have a coffee together. Or a drink, the pubs are still open.'

The street they were in now was mainly residential, but there were lights in the houses, a small general store that was still open, the vegetables set out on trestles on the pavement, and a group of cheerful people spilling out of a public house on the corner, talking and laughing. It seemed unlikely to Coral that she could be in danger in this well-lit, friendly neighbourhood. Her flutters of panic abated and she felt calm again, in control. She said, 'I could use a drink, come to think of it.'

He glanced at her, she thought with a puzzled look, as if he had forgotten he had a passenger. He had light brown eyes, the colour of pale tea, and thick brows, a few white wiry hairs bristling. He said, 'I don't drink.'

Coral said, 'Then let me out. Now. Please. I'll walk home.'

Apparently in response, he swerved across the road, reversed, and swung the car round. An oncoming car, which must have been close behind, flashed lights and blared horns as it crashed into the kerb, maybe into a lamppost—Coral heard the vicious metallic bang, and the shatter of breaking glass but saw nothing: she was being thrown around far too violently. Once the car leaped forward she was so grateful to be travelling in one direction again that for a moment she was too relieved to be frightened.

Then, as they reached the end of the street, she was terrified.

She clung to the dash as the car shot across the main road inches in front of a roaring red bus, only just missed a white van going the other way, and hurtled into a darker street than before, a long blank wall on one side, an apparently derelict block of flats on the other. She heard herself whimpering, gasping. 'Oh no, oh no, oh no . . .'

He said, 'Don't talk. I don't want to talk now.'

That silenced her. And, absurdly, the sudden roughness in his tone, the slight masculine coarseness that she had found attractive earlier, had the same effect now: she was suddenly charged with a sexual excitement, so sharpened by danger that she felt competent, powerful. She might be locked in a speeding car with a lunatic but she wasn't afraid. She could get herself out of this mess. She said, sternly, 'This has gone far enough. Stop the car and let me out. Now.'

That was the tone to take. No nonsense. Don't show fear. Don't beg. Don't even cajole. They were approaching a side road, a taxi waiting to turn out of it with its FOR HIRE sign shining out like a beacon. She said, 'If I'm quick, I can pick up that cab.'

He grunted and slammed on the brakes. She

flew forward, the pain, as she struck the windscreen, was intense, unbelievable; it seemed to grow until it filled her head; she could feel the shape of her skull, her jaw, all the bones of her face, etched with agony. She thought, My nose, I've broken my nose. She felt her forehead and her fingers came away sticky.

He said, in a perfectly ordinary, grumbling voice, 'Why on earth did you unfasten your seat-belt?'

*   *   *

Remembering that remark now, makes her think he was probably innocent of any evil intention. Unless he is mad, which is morally much the same thing. No malice intended.

She is almost certain that the concern he showed once he realised how much she was hurt was quite genuine. He had touched her face with gentle fingers and said no, he didn't think her nose was broken, quite authoritatively, as if he were a nurse or a doctor.

That bit of diagnosing had not been immediate. Immediately he had simply said, 'Oh, God,' and shot off, not driving so fast now, driving in fact quite skilfully and carefully, not looking at her but touching her leg once or twice, a couple of fatherly pats that seemed meant to be reassuring. She assumed

100

he was taking her to a hospital. She had no idea where they were and her anxieties about landing up in the same hospital as Will had not surfaced. She closed her eyes and felt herself slipping in and out of consciousness.

That's how she remembers it anyway. A nightmare dream sequence. Of course she should have kept her eyes open, tried to see where they were going, fix a landmark in her memory somehow, a street name, a tube station. But she had been shuddering and helpless with pain.

The car was slowing down, stopping. There was light glowing pinkly through her eyelids. She opened her stinging eyes and he was bending over her, touching her face with his skilful fingers. She must have asked him if her nose was broken, because she remembers him shaking his head and saying no, in that surprisingly confident voice. And then, 'All the same I think it calls for an ambulance.'

They were in an underground car park. Facing a concrete wall with numbers painted in yellow. The number of this bay was 7. The park was roughly half full of cars. Not an office block, then, not at this time of night. How late did National Car Parks stay open?

A grey, desolate, echoing place. A waste of concrete. People running, hiding, chasing each other. A film set . . .

Years ago she had played in a TV film, a girl on the run from a serial killer. She had been his first victim, only distantly glimpsed as she dodged between the cars in the subterranean car park, but later the camera had lingered on her dead body, head thrown back, blood slashing her neck, her clothes torn, one breast bare. Will had said, watching it with her, 'You make a handsome corpse, darling.'

Panic gripped her. Second-hand, self-induced, as she told herself; all the same she could feel herself suffocating. She blew into her cupped hands; an old actor's trick, a cure for stage fright. The man was getting out of the driver's seat, back turned towards her. She tried her door and it opened. Straight ahead, four or five bays away, a lit sign. EXIT. And the image of a pin man walking.

She was running. It jarred her face and head painfully; she could feel the swelling flesh shaking loose on her cheekbones. He shouted something behind her but she had reached the metal door. There was no handle, it was a heavy door; beyond it two more doors in a small lobby. One was a lift, no call button, only a locking device needing a key; the other door showed the pin man again, this time climbing stairs. But the first door was opening behind her. He said, 'What the hell are you doing?'

He was holding out his arm, stretching his hand to her. Pleading? She threw all her weight against the heavy metal door, knocking him backwards, and he yelped like a dog. Had she caught his hand? She said, absurdly,

'Sorry.'

She could hear him groaning. She ran, through the door with the climbing man, up concrete steps to the street. Another heavy door. On the other side of it, a notice said PRIVATE PARKING. NO ENTRANCE. Further down the street, to her left, was a brightly lit apartment block; presumably you could only get into the car park by an internal lift.

She hurried to her right, away from the apartment block, into darkness. Sleet stung her swelling face. She had no idea where she was; she looked for street signs that might show the postal district but found none. Then, turning a corner, coming to a humped bridge, she saw an overnight petrol station that seemed vaguely familiar, but all petrol stations looked alike, didn't they? This one was called Lock Side.

The bridge crossed a canal; over the low brick wall she could see houseboats moored. A street-lamp threw yellow light on crinkling brown water. When the children were young, she had taken them walking along the towpath, feeding the ducks, watching the narrow boats negotiate the lock. This lock? Was she so close to home?

She didn't recognise the handsome young Asian behind the pay desk at the petrol station but she thought the way the newspapers and groceries were displayed was familiar. The shop itself was closed, the door locked on the

103

inside, and the man made no move to open it. He looked at her through the window of the pay desk with a shuttered expression. Was this a rough area? Of course, she must look repellent. Alarmingly so. A victim of gang warfare?

She said, 'I've been in an accident. As you can see. I need to get home.'

He looked beyond her—for a lurking accomplice, perhaps. Then back at her, frowning. He said, with seeming reluctance, 'I can call a cab.'

He turned his back; either dialling or pressing a button. She could hear him speaking, though not what he said. He said, without looking at her, 'Ten minutes. Maybe quicker, depending on traffic.'

He moved away from the window and appeared to be absorbed in rearranging a rack of coloured magazines. She tapped on the window and said, 'Please let me come in. I'm so cold,' but was unsurprised when he ignored her. This was a lonely place at night.

She looked round her. There was no place to hide. Was it safe to wait here, in this brightly lit place? Suppose he came after her? Enraged because she had injured him. Oh, surely, even if he wouldn't let her into the shop, the Asian would call the police if she was attacked on his forecourt. But she was icy with fear . . .

She can remember now, two days later, how cold she had felt even though she cannot recreate the fear. She has always found it easier to act out emotions than to recall them, which may be a hazard of her profession: her own sensitivities frozen by fakery, as a manual labourer's hands are hardened by work. But she knows she was afraid in a way she had not been afraid since she was a child terrified of the tiger who hid on the dark upper floors of the house where she lived with her father and stepmother, waiting to pounce on her when she had to go upstairs to the lavatory.

It seems ridiculous now. The *man*—oh, she must give him a name, it would de-mystify him, make him human, not a sinister shadow, call him Velvet Cap—had not really threatened her. Once the minicab had turned up, whisked her home, she had tried to tell herself that the whole episode had been little more than ridiculous, her own reaction, hysterical. If she hadn't been left with the physical consequences, she would be making a dramatic tale out of it now, not quite a joke but dwelling on its funny side, portraying herself (without, of course, ever saying so) as admirably brave and calm, a (potentially) tragic heroine.

Would it have impressed Will? As things are, he will probably be angry that she hadn't told him before. That she hadn't been to a doctor. That she hadn't told the police . . .

She makes telephone calls. To Greg in Brighton, who is ritually sympathetic about the violent attack of flu that she claims made her incapable of speech earlier but will clearly never forgive her. To the hospital, leaving a message with the ward sister to ask her to tell Will she has not gone to Brighton after all and that she will be along to see him tomorrow. To Silas, to thank him for his message and to enquire after his health and ask if there is anything he wants her to buy for him. To Angela's mother to thank her for looking after Dinkie who can come home now if she wants to. And to Hannah about whom she feels guilty . . .

$$* \qquad * \qquad *$$

Hannah says, settling comfortably among the cushions of the sofa on which she and Julius usually position themselves with a glass of dry sherry while they watch the evening news, 'That was Coral, she's had a horrid fall and given herself a black eye, poor thing, so I didn't tell her about Clare's letter, insult to injury, I thought. It's disgraceful, the state of the pavements in her part of London. She didn't sound herself at all. I hope she'll be fit to look after Will when he comes out of hospital. Sometimes I wish we lived a bit closer. Though you'd miss the sheep, of course. But it would be nice to see the children more often. As well as my poor little brother.'

'If you want to see Will so badly,' Julius

says, 'why don't you go down to London? I know you'd rather not take the train on your own but I'll drive you if you like.'

He puts as much enthusiasm as he can manage into this offer, although he knows that Hannah knows how little he likes to drive on the motorway. Until very recently she enjoyed driving, for which he was grateful; he has never been happy with machines, he can't even manage an electric razor, and although he drives now it is only because he has to occasionally, living as they do out on the moors. Hannah's growing reclusiveness, her unwillingness not only to drive but to travel alone, baffles him. Some psychological disturbance, he assumes, but it would be unwise to suggest this; even to think of the outrage with which she would respond makes him feel weary. And, more important, it might alarm her; make her afraid she was going the same way as her mother.

He says, 'On the other hand we are going down for the birthday. Suppose we go a couple of days earlier? We don't have to stay with anyone, we can afford an hotel. You could spend time with Will, maybe buy yourself something new for the lunch. You don't have to endure a department store. There are lots of small shops in Knightsbridge or Bond Street.'

'Smart shops. I'm too old and shabby' Hannah shakes her head complacently. Then frowns, hurt and aggrieved: 'I was going to wear that blue thing, I thought you liked it.'

'I just thought, something new,' Julius says hastily. 'But the blue is fine.'

The soap that precedes the six o'clock news is ending; Julius turns up the sound and says, 'Now for the Happy Hour.'

Hannah sits back and meekly sips her sherry. Julius likes to watch the news uninterrupted and Hannah has always indulged him. In return he sits patiently beside her through what are, to him, interminable programmes about wild animals. Hannah is enraptured by lions and tigers and bears, the larger they are, the more savage, the better. Julius finds the feeding habits of lions, which these programmes often linger upon, especially upsetting. He can envisage them stalking the Yorkshire moors, leaping upon his beautiful Hampshire Downs sheep and tearing their throats out. Luckily, since wildlife films are considered educational for children, the gory scenes he dislikes are usually shown quite early in the evening and he can make the excuse of disappearing to the kitchen to make dinner.

He does not know that Hannah is often as distressed by the television news as he is by her favourite programmes. She is aware of what goes on in the world, she listens to the World Service, she works for Amnesty International as a volunteer, and subscribes to Médecin Sans Frontières and Oxfam, but she shrinks from filmed scenes of misery and carnage. She has never told Julius how she feels because she despises herself for what she considers a shamefully pampered, self-regarding sensitivity.

But she is glad to escape from the screen when the telephone rings, even though it is Silas. Although Hannah loves her father he has always made her feel clumsy. When she was a girl she knew he was disappointed in her; in her appearance and her loud, awkward manner. She had imagined that as she grew older and he became frailer, he might come to appreciate her concern for him and come to love her more. Instead, now she has turned seventy, an old woman with rheumaticky joints and whiskers on her chin, *he* seems as hearty as ever, and almost to resent her loving advice and enquiries. He should be taking more care of himself, travelling a bit less, eating more sensibly. The last time she and Julius saw him in London, about nine months ago, he had eaten an enormous meal: roast beef well marbled with fat, extra butter on his potatoes, the whole plateful smothered in salt. Ice cream for dessert, a great plateful of cheese, no fruit, not a single green vegetable. She had tried to explain to him—trying to make a little joke of it—that this was not exactly the healthiest diet for a man of his age, but he had not appeared to have heard her. He had complained that his hearing-aid was hurting him, taken it out and put it (very deliberately, it had seemed to her) on the white tablecloth, beside his plate. There had been no more real communication between them that evening, though he had become unusually affectionate when they had left him, pressing Julius's hand with both of his own, and kissing her on both cheeks. And as they had left the club she had looked back and seen him leaning on his sticks and looking after them, she thought with a sad, yearning expression . . .

It had made her cry.

Silas says, 'That you, Julius?'

'Hannah, Father. It's *Hannah*.'

'Oh. Hannah, is it?'

'Yes, Father. Haven't you got that amplifier thing on the telephone?'

'Whassay? Never mind that. D'you get my letter?'

'Clare's letter, you mean. Yes, I did get it, Father. Most affecting. How are you? Taking good care of yourself, I do hope.'

'That's one thing you don't have to do, once you get to my age,' Silas says. His hearing apparently fully restored, he speaks remarkably crisply. 'I've been thinking, Hannah, about the evolution of tools. Take the tin opener. 1810 when a wrought iron can was introduced, tin-coated of course, and meant for the armed forces, so no one bothered too much about how the food was to be got out of the tin. Soldiers had bayonets and knives. Even when tinned food was on sale to civilians, round about the 1820's there was no proper tool. You needed a hammer and chisel. There was a can opener patented, Ezra Warner in 1858 is my memory, a kind of bayonet with a curved blade, but you could cut yourself on the jagged edge of the tin and you needed a strong wrist, not for ladies. Of course there have been a good many ways of opening tins since, the church key for one, and those pull-tab devices, not much good for weak fingers and you can still cut yourself. So there isn't yet what you might call a definitive tool almost two centuries after the first meat was tinned for the Army. Have you thought of that, Hannah?'

She says, weakly, 'No, Father. You must be right. How interesting.'

'No, no, no.' Silas sounds irritated suddenly. 'I'm talking about evolution, girl. The evolution of tools. And d'you know what my conclusion is?'

Hannah shakes her head. She says, 'You tell me, Father.'

A pause. Silas says harshly, 'Don't indulge me, I'm not senile yet. My conclusion is that evolution is *failure driven*. I've been giving a lot of thought to it lately. Same thing is true of almost anything you can mention. Zip fasteners for one. You have to strive, Hannah. Discontent leads to progress. That's what I mean by failure driven.'

And he puts down the telephone.

CHAPTER NINE

Silas says, after he has put the telephone
down, 'Typical Effie!'

And one of his rages erupts: suddenly, out
of the blue. This is something that has been
happening recently and, very occasionally,
when the volcano of anger has spent itself, he
worries that he is not in control any longer.
Mostly, however, he feels he is justified.

As he does now. Dismissing Hannah,
replacing her with her mother.

Effie would never *listen*. He had not
expected her to help in the business as some
wives did whose husbands were shopkeepers.
But she had as good a head for figures as he
did and there were times, after Arnold Pepys
had retired altogether, when he could have
done with some accounting help in the
evenings. But she didn't offer and he wouldn't
ask. It was the price he paid, he thought
sometimes, for marrying a lady rather than a
young woman who had grown up expecting to
earn her living.

But he had hoped she would listen.

*   *   *

Since Bella's death, Silas has become a
traveller in time. He sits with a book on his

112

lap—he doesn't want to be seen as an old man, dreaming—and allows his mind to run free. He sees—*feels*—his past life as a vast, echoing tunnel, or underground cave. He journeys through it and around it, mining the seam of his personal history; hidden or half-forgotten events barely glimpsed out of the corner of an eye, a brief flash of light in the darkness, others dwelt upon, constantly revisited, permanently lit. He can traverse a decade in a matter of seconds or linger for days on a single moment, in one particular room. And although sometimes, conscientiously, he sets himself to review his working life, the establishment of his chain of ironmongers, his pleasure in each individual shop with his name engraved in the glass transom over the door, his one regret, when he sold up the company, that the Edinburgh lawyer was no longer alive to be impressed by how much his despised son-in-law had turned out to be worth, the times he returns to most often are fuelled by more personal emotions; happiness, anger and pain.

He remembers Hannah's birth chiefly as the occasion of severe disappointment. He had tickets for the first voyage from London to Scotland of Nigel Greeley's *Flying Scotsman*. Silas had fallen in love with the engine at the British Empire Exhibition three years earlier and promised himself this once-in-a-lifetime treat. Even if he knew in his heart that Effie, almost eight months pregnant, had only really

113

agreed to go with him because she wanted to see her mother and father in Edinburgh, a last visit before the baby arrived, he hoped that speeding through England she might come to feel the wonder of engineering as he did, its awesome power and purpose. But she went into labour five weeks early and Hannah was born at the same time as the *Flying Scotsman* drew into Edinburgh Waverley ahead of schedule.

Silas had put off replacing the Arnold Pepys signs outside the shops around Norwich in case the child was a boy. Silas Mudd and Son. But when the baby girl was placed in his arms he felt nothing but a flood of awestruck love for this small, red-faced person who had not been in the world half an hour ago, and was now his responsibility. Effie smiled at him happily, and his heart ached with joy. He loved his wife, he loved his new daughter. All was well.

Until later that evening. The doctor and the midwife had gone. The monthly nurse had taken the baby to sleep in her room. He and Effie were alone in their bedroom that was still scented by the lavender twigs the nurse had burned in the hearth to conceal the smell of birthing and blood. Lily was finishing her long day's work in the kitchen beneath them with her usual noisy energy; as she riddled the boiler and made it up for the night, the sound travelled up the wall to their bedroom.

'What a row she does make, how on earth does she do it?' Effie said—smiling, not fretful. Lily's heavy-handed, heavy-footed, heavy-breathing behaviour was a running joke between them. A skinny, frail-looking young woman, she behaved and moved like a large one; when she walked across the floor of her attic bedroom above them, it was as if an elephant danced overhead. But she was willing and cheerful and although Silas found it uncomfortable to have a stranger in his house all the time, and took care to be decently dressed before he left his bedroom, he understood that Effie, who was used to servants, found it perfectly natural to wander about the house in her underclothes, that as far as she was concerned Lily was not to be considered as a person with ideas and feelings who might be shocked or embarrassed. Effie often left the bathroom door open when she was sitting on the lavatory and Silas sometimes thought she would not even care if Lily should enter the bedroom while they were in bed, making love. He always locked the door against this contingency and Effie laughed at him for it. Who on earth could come in? For her Lily was nobody, nothing, not really *there.*

When they moved to Norwich, Silas had imagined Effie would want a daily help, a young woman still living at home with her family like the girl they had employed in their first, rented house in Wymondham but Effie's mother, who had travelled from Scotland as soon as she knew her daughter was pregnant to organise and advise, had dismissed this idea with laughter and scorn. How did he think poor darling Effie could manage without a proper maid? Who would lay and light the fire before she got up in the morning? Who would make breakfast?

'It's no good your saying you'll do it, Silas,' said his mother-in-law, with a curtly dismissive wave of her hand and a vicious grin. 'I know *men*!'

When he thinks of Effie's mother, Silas wonders what can have happened to make her hate his sex so unconditionally. He had thought at the time it was only him she disliked, a tradesman, below the salt, her unfortunate daughter's bad bargain, but nowadays, when he happens upon her in the course of his armchair wanderings, he seems to see her more clearly than he did when she was a living thorn in his side. What he sees now is a handsome woman with a bitter mouth who had never been satisfied; a clever woman who had never been properly *used*. Silas is unsure what he means by this. He doesn't go on to reflect that she might have been happier and less disagreeable if she had been given a chance to exercise her mind and her energy outside the huge and cavernous Edinburgh apartment where she kept house for the Writer to the Signet. He merely notes that she was *too clever for her own good*, a perfectly adequate explanation to his mind for the resentment she clearly felt towards every adult male who came near her.

Silas reckons he was her favourite target. He can remember every word of their wounding exchanges as clearly as if they had taken place no more than an hour ago. (More clearly, in fact. His short-term memory is shot: he often forgets what he did yesterday.) He had paid three hundred and forty-five pounds for the Norwich house in which Hannah was born, a proud purchase that had shocked Aunt who had rented all her life; five shillings a week for her cottage in the year of Hannah's birth. 'This huge house,' Aunt had said, impressed but fearful. 'Suppose the roof leaks. Or the chimney blows off. It's a great responsibility, Silas.'

His mother-in-law had a different opinion. Standing in the hallway, smartly costumed, hatted and gloved, she had said, 'I daresay it will have to do, though I must say it's not a house I would care to bring a new baby into. The lino is cracked in the bathroom. I suppose one ought to be grateful there *is* a bathroom!'

And she had laughed her sneering laugh, her angry eyes snapping.

She had been more tactful with Effie. 'It's a funny little house, dear, I know you're good at making the best of things, but how *will* you manage with only three bedrooms? I know the girl can sleep in the attic, but when you get a nanny for Little X, Nanny will want her own room I would think.'

'We'll have to manage without a spare room, Mother,' Effie had said—warming Silas's heart with what he saw as her gallant defence of him. 'If you want to come and stay you'll have to make do. We're going to get a Put-U-Up for the drawing room.'

A nanny had not yet been engaged, nor been mentioned by Effie throughout her pregnancy. When Gladys Ogilvie came tomorrow, as she had insisted on doing as soon as Silas had telephoned the news of Hannah's arrival, even though he had also been able to tell her the monthly nurse was free to come at short notice, the small third bedroom next to the nursery would still be empty. After Lily had pounded up the stairs to bed and the boards were cracking and creaking above them, Effie said, 'I ought to have done something about Mother's room. Well, of course, I thought I'd have more time.' She looked wan and exhausted suddenly. 'Flowers. I was going to buy some nice soap. And she'll need a chamber-pot. She won't want to come out of her room at night to go to the bathroom. I think there's a pot in the attic cupboard. We'll have to ask Lily tomorrow.'

She looked as if she were going to cry. Silas took her hands and rubbed them gently. 'I'll use the outside lavatory while she's here,' he said. 'That leaves just three people for the bathroom, your mother and you and the nurse. And I'll wash and shave in the scullery. So no one need be embarrassed.' He smiled at her, amused by a sudden vision of his mother-in-law squatting, scrawny bottom bared, on a china chamber-pot. He added, hastily, in case Effie could see into his mind, 'As long as Lily doesn't object to my sharing her toilet arrangements, that is.'

'Why should Lily mind? Why are you grinning in that silly way, Silas?'

'I don't know. Nothing. Just happy. Look, I'll get some flowers first thing tomorrow. And soap. Whatever you want. So don't worry. Come on now, you smile at *me* . . .'

She turned her head restlessly. 'It's all so difficult. I should have done something . . . it's not my fault the baby came early . . .'

'Of course it isn't, darling . . .'

He thought, This is an important occasion. Their first child had been born; they were a proper family now. He ought to do something, say something worthy of this moment. Tomorrow *she* would be here, Effie's termagant mother, criticising, complaining, and there would be no peace, no chance, to give voice to the emotions that ached and throbbed inside him like a fever. He and Effie were alone, as they might not be for a long time, and all they could talk about was where her mother was going to wash her face and empty her bladder.

But what should he say to her? He and Effie had only been married ten months. The wonder of being with her, finding her there when he came home in the evening, waking up in the morning to her sweet, sleeping face on the pillow beside him, had been enough happiness, all he wanted. Sometimes she read in the evenings, she was what she called 'a great reader', and he would never interrupt or disturb her, being content just silently to watch her, at first curled like a kitten in her armchair and, later, lying with her feet on a footstool, her book propped on the firm swell of her pregnancy. When they talked, it was about themselves, how amazing that they had found each other, how threadbare their lives had been during those long years apart. He told her how he had dreamed of her, waking and sleeping; she told him how she had listened for the postman, and crept down the stairs to the hall before her parents were up. 'Even cold mornings, oh, such a shiver, barefoot, in my nightie'—a sly combination of girlish silliness and sexual teasing, that drove Silas wild with lust and love.

Now, this evening, the obvious, happy solution was barred to him. There must be another way to be close to her, to blow away the dark cloud of her mother's arrival that seemed to be threatening him. He wished he had read some of the novels she found so engrossing. Or paid more attention when she had prattled on about friends and neighbours. Aunt disapproved of gossip, and since he didn't want Aunt to disapprove of his darling, he had tried to close his ears.

He saw that she might find his interests narrow. Defined as simply as possible, he saw them as man conquering nature. Lindbergh flying the Atlantic, the *Flying Scotsman* reaching a speed of a hundred miles an hour. Perhaps, if he turned to something more homely, domestic, she might understand what he found so fascinating not only about engineering triumphs, great bridges and locomotives, but tools of all kinds. Knives and forks. Can-openers. Hammers.

Silas said, 'Did you know, darling, that Karl Marx was astonished to find how many different hammers were made in Birmingham in the 1860s? Five hundred different kinds of hammer! And yet, when you think about it, there are probably about five hundred jobs you need a hammer for. If you tried to do those five hundred jobs with the same hammer, you would be frustrated four hundred and ninety-nine times. That's how inventions come about. People trying to get the right tool for the job. And failing. And trying again.'

'What are you talking about?' Effie, for a moment, had her mother's look, a pinched mouth, almost a sneer.

But it was only a trick of the light. In fact,

she was smiling indulgently. Silas said, 'Think of a stool. Not so many different kinds of stool as there are different kinds of hammers, but there's one I like the name of. It's called Nobody. It started off as a piece of plank with a hole in the middle and one leg. It's a potter's stool. I've not used it myself but I once watched a potter. He sat on the Nobody and it swayed with him as he swayed as he worked the clay. Someone invented that stool just by chance. It's how things get invented and change.'

Effie was looking drained and weary again. 'Oh, Siley,' she said. 'Siley.'

She sounded like his mother now. It frightened him. He said, 'Don't call me that. Please.'

*   *   *

Silas only visits, thinks of, his mother occasionally—or, more exactly, she only returns to haunt him occasionally There was a time in adolescence when she regularly appeared in his dreams, wearing a loose white shift and bleeding from the mouth. He would wake from these nightmares in a torment of guilt. Could he have saved her? If he hadn't wasted time hauling her up on the bed? Even a four-year-old should have known better. Screamed for help the moment he found her. Or earlier still, known she was miserable, tried to help her. Told Molly. His father.

Aunt had never told him what killed her. Just, 'Poor soul was tired to death, dear. just think of her at rest now. And remember she loved you.'

You didn't question Aunt. In the main she was open, argumentative, given to boisterous expression of opinions—some of them considered outrageous in a small country town, at that time—but she had unexpected areas of reticence, and he learned to respect them. He knew, by a tremor of her eyelids, a slight jerk of the chin, that he—or someone else—had ventured too close, touched some hidden weakness. His mother's death was one. His father's failure as a husband and father, another. In the years after his return from America until his death just after Alice was born, Aunt treated Henry Mudd as the head of her household, deferring to his judgement in all worldly matters, home politics, foreign affairs, always giving him the *Manchester Guardian* in the mornings, neatly folded, before she had looked at it.

She even polished his boots for him. When Silas made a mild, jokey comment (you didn't criticise Aunt!) she pursed her lips and instead of replying to him, spoke to her pet chicken on the cushion by the fire. 'People have to have something to keep their pride up, don't they, my chick?'

Silas was glad that Aunt had someone to

help her in the house now her arthritis was bothering her, and at least Henry Mudd carried coals, dug the garden. But he felt nothing for his father beyond family responsibility, and because he was ashamed of his indifference, made punctilious efforts whenever he visited to spend some time alone with him: although Aunt did her best to treat her brother with the respect she insisted was due to him, she became impatient if she had to try too hard for too long, and she would fall to making irritable puffing sounds, little snorts through her nose, pointed sighs. But Henry and Silas had little in common. Henry was passionate about the theatre and the cinema. One of his recent enthusiasms was for the films of Laurel and Hardy, which was a mystifying taste to Silas, and Henry's close reading of the *Manchester Guardian* tended to make him pronounce, with what seemed to Silas a rather pompously authoritative air, on events at home and abroad.

It did not occur to Silas that his father might have been nervous of him, that he was merely trying to keep his end up when he asked his son if he had read about Mahatma Gandhi's march to the sea and what effect he thought it would have on the British Government, and announced, without waiting for an answer, that 'my paper' had said that 'of course' Gandhi only represented a small section of India and the campaign for civil disobedience had found no support in the National Assembly.

Silas listened politely and nodded. The next time he came, bringing Effie and Hannah, he read the *Manchester Guardian* from cover to cover before settling his wife and daughter in the Invicta for the drive to Swaffham. Hannah screamed and struggled on her mother's lap for much of the journey, kicking Silas with her hard little shoes, behaviour that Effie, who resented 'wasting' a day on an opinionated old woman and a drained, useless old man, endured in martyred silence. By the time Aunt and Effie had taken Hannah out for a walk, and Silas was settled beside the fire with his father, the only piece of information he remembered clearly from his filial homework was a brief paragraph about an eight-year-old boy in Newcastle who had been brought to the infirmary with a steel ring jammed tight on one finger. Steel saws, files, even carborundum, failed to remove it. Then, at an engineer's suggestion, the child's finger was placed on a fourteen-pound sledge-hammer and the ring, on being struck by another hammer of the same weight, split open at once.

'Amazing, don't you think, Dad?'

Henry Mudd was sitting with his back to the lace-curtained window. Except for the fire flicker, his face was in shadow. He seemed to be flinching away, one shoulder hunched up protectively. Puzzled, Silas thought to begin with. Or hurt, perhaps? Did his father think he

125

was mocking him?

He said, uncertainly, 'It wouldn't have hurt the boy, Dad. Just a light tap.'

Henry Mudd was shaking his head and muttering.

Silas said, 'Do you know what carborundum is, Dad? I didn't know, had to look it up. It's silicon carbide, used for cutting and grinding. just another tool.'

But it was neither sensitivity nor ignorance that was troubling Henry. He gave a deep, shuddering sigh. He said, 'I don't know why I'm still here.'

*   *   *

For Silas, nowadays, his father is always sitting in that chair, in that room. He must have seen him in his last months, after the stroke had confined him to the high brass bed in the back bedroom, but all he clearly remembers about that time is his concern for Aunt who, to begin with, had insisted on doing everything for her brother herself, feeding him, cleaning him, shaving him, washing his soiled sheets, only allowing Silas to employ a nurse to sit with him for a few hours at night after several exhausting weeks, and even then, very reluctantly.

'Nurses,' she said, with contempt. 'I'd have thought you'd have finished with nurses after what happened with Hannah!'

She had a habit, Aunt, of finishing arguments with incontrovertible statements that did not always bear much examination. After two disturbed, screaming nights, Hannah had 'settled'—Gladys Ogilvie's word, as if her granddaughter were some sort of jelly—and become a quiet, peaceful baby, sleeping between feeds, round the clock. Silas had been relieved, for Effie's sake naturally, but also because it had meant that his mother-in-law had taken herself off back to Edinburgh after only ten days, much sooner than he had feared. 'That's a good easy baby, you've been *very lucky*,' she had said, as Silas drove her to the railway station—her deliberate emphasis implying, he felt, that any child he had fathered was more likely to have been some kind of creature from hell. Two weeks later, when the departing monthly nurse said to Effie, 'If she cries, just put a flannel on the gas a few minutes and pop it on her face for a while, then you get a nice, placid baby,' he had begged Effie not to pass on this piece of professional advice to her mother. But he had told Aunt, of course.

He said to Aunt, five years later, when his father was dying and his second daughter just born, that he really didn't think the two cases were comparable; one at the beginning of life, the other at the end. Indeed, he almost went on to say, if the monthly nurse who had looked after Hannah were to employ the same methods to comfort his dying old father as she had used to quieten baby Hannah, it might be no bad thing. But Aunt was not much given to black humour so he held his tongue.

She said, 'That dreadful woman. At least I made sure she never came in contact with another innocent baby, at least not in this town, and the doctor promised he'd spread the word. You can't be certain, mind you, people in the same profession stick together, but I've never let him forget it, you can be quite sure of that.'

Silas remembers exactly the tone of her voice and the time and place of this conversation. It was four o'clock in the afternoon and he was sitting with Aunt in the small back living room with the wooden stair rising up; Silas on the settle and Aunt in her old rocking chair. Creak, creak, back and forth, the fire crackling, the light flooding in from the open door to the scullery, the musty-smelling geraniums wintering on the window-sill. This is the room Silas visits almost every day now he is old; he suspects Aunt would prefer him to look for her in the parlour, with the best china set out on the lace tablecloth, but he knows he can always be certain of finding her in this more workaday room. And he often needs to find her. Her energy, her moral certainties comfort him still. And her goodness. He is sure of her goodness: it has been a measurement to him throughout his life. He hasn't wiped out her old age, he is happy and proud that she allowed him to see she was properly cared for, in her own home, to the end, but he prefers to summon her up, remember her when she was younger, in the energetic and confident bustle of her middle years. When she was Aunt-in-a-hurry, shouting at him to polish his boots, clean his teeth, placing bowls of steaming porridge on the table for breakfast. Or Aunt-the-headmistress setting off to school, thick woollen skirt clipped to the guard on her bicycle to preserve her modesty in the high winds that swept this part of Norfolk in winter, a bag of books slung on one side of the handlebars, a bag of potatoes on the other. (She took potatoes to school all winter long, to bake in the stove for the children who came to school hungry.) Or Aunt-the-protector-and-comforter, rough hands, loud voice, broad, warm lap.

When he was young, before he went to the grammar school and Molly went off to London, his sister was often in that room too, not always at home in the evenings, sometimes staying with girlfriends in Norwich, but Silas can see her there whenever he wants to, sitting at the round walnut table that was the only piece of furniture saved from the bailiffs when they left the house in Walthamstow, fair hair falling forward in a shining curtain as she gets on with her homework, or writes in her diary, the diary of an About-to-Be-Famous Actress, or learns her part for the school play.

And very rarely, involuntarily, he sees and hears his father: Henry Mudd, shortly before the stroke felled him, sitting in the same room in front of the lace-curtained window, flinching away as if he feared his son might be going to strike him and saying, 'I don't know why I'm still here.'

*   *   *

Silas has said the same thing to Bella. Lying in bed together, in her chilly Greek house on the harbour, his old bones stiff and aching, but not mentioning the discomfort because she was coughing so wretchedly. They had put off going to Athens to re-make her will because she had caught this bad cold, and when they were forced to go two days later neither of them was in any state to speak to a lawyer.

That night in bed, trying to comfort her, strong old arm round her, Silas had wondered if the iron bands tightening round his own chest, the pain in his lungs, might be going to finish him. Not before time, he said silently, eighty-six years is enough for any man, and then, aloud, 'I don't know why I'm still here.' Not remembering, until he had spoken them as a wry joke, that he had heard those words years before, not long after Hannah was born, spoken by his useless old father.

Prophetic? 'Hope not,' he said, is sure that

he said; the last thing he can recall before the spine-jolting misery of the ambulance, the incredible anguish of breathing, the only comfort Bella's hand holding his. He thought, Should her hand be so cold? He managed to croak, 'You all right, Belle?' Slipping away from her then, not waiting, not able to wait, for her answer, unable to speak again because the oxygen mask was pressing down on his face, fighting it, imagining someone was trying to kill him. 'Is this death?' he thought he said, sure that it must be, consciously thinking, Not sorry, either, and remembering nothing more until he woke in the hospital, feeling weak and tired but much better, soon be strong as a horse again, Bella beside him, sitting on the bed, pulling the covers uncomfortably taut over him, stroking him, murmuring. Soft, silly, loving words, comforting . . .

Then he slept, and when he woke she was still sitting there, not on the bed but in an armchair beside it, and he thought she had fallen asleep. He called out to her but she didn't move and before he rang the bell for the nurse he knew that she must be dead.

A massive heart-attack. That was a shock; he felt she had cheated him. Letting him make all those financial arrangements on the assumption she was bound to survive him. 'You'll be my relict,' he had said, 'that's the legal term,' meaning to make her laugh, when his side of the business had all been signed and finished in London. She should have told him then what a bad risk she was; to keep silent in a matter of this kind was the same as lying directly.

She was no better than a thief. And a tramp too, no doubt. For a while after her death, brooding over how she'd deceived him about her health, Silas thought of those gigolos on the cruise where he'd met her, Gentlemen Hosts they were called, employed to dance with the single ladies, no hanky-panky allowed, so she'd told him, but he remembered the way she had behaved towards the ones she had danced with, smiling when they came near, winking, rolling her lovely eyes . . . how open she was to every man she met, any man who so much as looked at her . . .

There was a moment he had almost told Will what a slut she was, what a liar, luckily he'd had enough sense to stop himself, known in his heart he was wrong, that a lot of his anger was grief and once it had spent itself he would remember how happy she'd made him. He was fairly sure that Aunt would have disapproved of Bella, thought her idle and frivolous, but in her company he had discovered an ease, a lightness of spirit he had not known before.

And she had not only made him laugh but made him feel witty. Calling up one occasion, when she was parading naked and pink from her bath, before the looking-glass in some hotel (he cannot be bothered to search his mind or his diaries for the exact location) he remembers her unselfconsciously charting the decline of her body. 'I used to have pretty arms, now look at them, all baggy and droopy.' But then, without pause, she had lifted those same baggy arms high over her head, pulled in her stomach, and said, with obvious pleasure, 'Though not a bad figure for a woman of my age, wouldn't you say?'

And Silas had answered, on cue, 'Or for a man of mine!' A simple piece of repartee that had dissolved her in laughter at the time and makes him smile now.

He thinks, You might have been quite a lad, Silas my boy, if you had met Bella earlier!

And yet, he doesn't miss Bella now as he still misses Effie. He knows this is perverse: when he summons up Effie he is rarely comforted as he is when he spends time with Bella. Now he has forgiven his second wife for her heart-attack, she makes a cheerful if ghostly companion; he talks to her most days about whatever comes into his mind, the state of his bowels, the pills Davey has given him for the cramps that wake him at night, what he ate for dinner, how the children are doing, especially her children, Davey and Clare, assuming, naturally, that she would be more interested in them than in his children, but also finding he has more to say about them because they appeal to him, not more than

Will, whom he loves, but more than Hannah or Alice. This is partly vanity, he admits it. Bella's children, so much younger than his elderly daughters, give him the illusion of being around twenty years younger himself. And Davey's children, still babies, are not yet at the stage of disappointing their parents as it is clear Alice's and Hannah's children are beginning to do.

Clare, of course, with her warm, open nature, reminds him of Bella, whereas neither of his daughters has any connection with Effie. Is this why Effie is lost to him, why he cannot bring her to life except as a hazy image that always seems to reproach him?

He resents the pain and the guilt he feels when she enters his mind. Resents her for being the cause of it.

But he still misses her, aches for her. Or aches for his younger self, who loved her and trusted her.

He wonders if his children's marriages are happy. None of his business, of course, a kind of voyeurism, Aunt would have called it *bad manners.* But Aunt is not to know what he is thinking and, in fact, what has begun to fascinate him just lately is not how little he knows about his own children but how little anyone knows about those who are close to them. He could spend his days summoning the roll-call of his dead but if he questions them they won't answer him, any more than they would have answered him when they were alive. Suppose he had said to Hannah just now, 'Are you happy, my daughter?' would she have answered him?

You'd get a better response from someone you met on a bus or in an airport lounge. Sitting in the bar of his club, in the corner, Silas says, aloud, 'Ask any passing stranger and you'll get a better answer,' and gets to his feet, grumbling, looks for his sticks, and makes his slow way to bed.

CHAPTER TEN

'What on earth have you done to yourself?' Will says.

He sounds more fretful and less concerned than a loving partner should. His defence, if he were to think he needed one, would be that he had been woken at three in the morning by the man in the next bed who had been seized with a wild bout of coughing, drawing breath only very occasionally and with a thin, screaming cry that was terrible to hear. No one in the ward had managed a proper look at this man, the curtains had remained drawn round his bed since he had been brought in, and when the emergency team arrived, the other patients turned their heads or hauled themselves up, depending on their degree of mobility, to get the best view they could. He had been rushed away on his squeaking and rattling bed before anyone could get a good look at him, and obviously no one could get back to sleep with the drama unresolved.

'He's been taken to another ward where we can do a bit more for his breathing,' the night sister said, 'nothing to worry about, this isn't *ER* or whatever you call it. If anyone feels they would like a cup of tea I'll be happy to make it.'

Which satisfied nobody. When she had returned to the nurse's station Will, who had been told by the consultant late last night that he was to leave in the morning, hospital beds being scarce in this flu-ridden winter, said it was typical of the NHS, treating a ward full of grown men as if they were one of the lower forms in a primary school. John, the skeleton in the bed opposite, added, with unsuitable relish, that he'd heard on the grapevine there was no room in intensive care. Presumably, since it was clearly this hospital's policy not to have noisy deathbeds in open wards, their unfortunate friend would be shut away in a spare cupboard and allowed to croak well out of earshot. Mr Thornley and Will glanced at each other with raised eyebrows, but as it was known that the skeleton was waiting for a terminal bed in a hospice, neither of them liked to say anything.

At five thirty, stewed and sugared tea was

brought round on a trolley, the lights were switched on and the pretence that any patient was likely to sleep again was officially abandoned. By eleven thirty, which is thirty minutes later than the time Will has asked Coral to come and collect him, he has been awake for eight hours and sitting on his bed, fully dressed, for five and a half of them. He has finished the books and the manuscripts he brought with him into the hospital, all of which were unsatisfactory in one way or another, and the newsagent, who does a round of the wards most days, has not come this morning.

In these circumstances, the appearance of his wife turns him from a balanced, kindly man in his middle years into a fractious child. Wicked Coral (who abandoned him here, against his will, in this horrible place) is wearing a black patch over one eye as if she is trying to make mock not only of him but of all the other poor invalids incarcerated here. More upsetting still, as she approaches he sees the purple bruising spreading around the patch, swelling over her cheekbone. And blurts out his question. *What on earth have you done to yourself?* Adding, 'No wonder you cancelled Brighton!'

He realises, as soon as he's spoken, just how oafish he sounds. Trying to put this right, he attempts a joke. 'Sorry, I thought for a minute you'd come to give me the old Black Spot.' Coral looks blank. He says, forcing jollity,

'*Treasure Island.* Old Blind Pugh! Seriously, darling. What on earth happened?'

She shakes her head, smiling ruefully 'It's a long story. Tell you later. Sorry I'm late. The traffic is dreadful.'

'Have you seen a doctor?' She keeps that silly smile on her face. Admitting her guilt. Will explodes, 'Christ, Coral! How irresponsible can you get? Look, go down to Casualty right now. Don't bother about me. I've waited long enough already, I can wait a bit longer. Or get a taxi home.'

'There are about a hundred people in Casualty, I looked as I came in, I knew what you'd say, you see! Broken legs, motor accidents, children who've swallowed poison. I don't somehow think I'd get much priority. And I've got the car on a meter that's about to expire.'

She bends, brushes a formal kiss on his forehead and picks up his small suitcase and his London Library bag full of unsatisfactory reading material. Then she smiles properly, at him, at the rest of the ward. 'Well,' she says, 'be a good boy, say goodbye nicely.'

Will is astonished. Coral is not usually arch. He says, 'Give me the books, they're too heavy.' He takes the bag from her. He has already said his farewell to each of his hospital friends individually. It is unlikely he will ever set eyes on any one of them ever again. He thinks he will miss them. He says, 'Well, once again, good luck, everyone. Maybe see you next winter.'

As a merry quip this falls flat. Only the skeleton grins, with a nice touch of malice. Mr Thornley nods gravely The handsome young Somali looks with more interest at Coral, who beams back in a motherly, or big-sisterly, way. A little nurse comes into the wing and takes the suitcase from Coral. 'I'll carry that down for you,' she says. 'I'm going to the ground floor.' Then, with a shy look at Will, 'We'll be sorry to lose your nice husband.'

* * *

As they walk to the lift, Coral is terrified suddenly. Her hands are greasy with sweat. No reason why he should be here, visiting times are afternoons and evenings; mornings are busy with doctor's rounds, admissions, departures. But Velvet Cap, she is sure, is not a man who pays much attention to rules.

Comes and goes as he pleases in that swirling coat.

Like a highwayman.

The curiously romantic image that rises in front of her, makes her feel hot and cold, shivery. A mixture of fear and sexual excitement.

She says quickly, 'Sure you're all right, Will? You didn't bully them into letting you go? You know what you are sometimes.'

She doesn't know why she says this. Will is always careful of his health. She corrects that sentence with an uneasy glance at her husband as if he might have stepped into her mind and heard it as a criticism. What she means is, Will is *sensible*. He would never discharge himself from a hospital. When he is told to stay at home, or in bed, he does as he's told. He always eats properly. Plenty of fruit and vegetables. He doesn't smoke any longer and only very rarely drinks too much. If he is given antibiotics he takes the full course and always eats yoghurt at the same time because their GP once told him that it counteracts the side-effects of the drugs.

He takes her hand. 'Sorry I was a pig. You know what it's like waiting. I'm horribly sorry about your eye. Did you fall?'

Why doesn't she just say, 'I got a lift home from the hospital last time I came, someone visiting another patient, and he/she braked too hard at a traffic light. Or a crossroad. Or a pedestrian crossing'?

But that would leave too many questions dangling. 'Why the hell didn't he/she drive you to a doctor, a hospital? What sort of person, for Christ's sake?'

She has told Dinkie, who has been staying with her friend in Thornhill Road but will be home this afternoon after school, that she tripped over a loose paving stone; she doesn't want the child to be too shocked when she sees

140

her. She said the same thing to Hannah. If she tells Will the truth, he will understand why she lied to his sister, though not why she lied to Dinkie, perhaps. Telling their daughter the truth might have underlined the usual parental warning. Don't accept lifts from strange men.

On the other hand, the whole truth might be better. Always easier than telling a half-truth, or a lie. Why can't she explain that she had thought she'd been kidnapped and was grateful to get away before she was murdered or raped?

But why hadn't she gone to the police in that case, as soon as she'd made her escape? Will might accept that she was too frightened and confused, in too much pain at the time, but he is bound to insist that she call the local station now, as soon as they get home. He will point out, quite rightly, that it is her citizen's duty. The man is a menace. Some other woman might not be so lucky. He will refuse to go to bed and rest as he should until she has done what he thinks she should do, working himself into a lather of indignation and fear. It is all his fault for having a weak immune system! Even if he did catch pneumonia, he should never have allowed himself to go into hospital. He should have been there when she needed him!

Will likes to blame himself. Coral is not sure she can bear this just at the moment.

She tucks her free hand through the crook

of Will's arm. 'Just the silliest accident. I ran across the road, lost my balance somehow on the pavement. I suppose there may have been some loose stones. Or a brick. You know that house on the corner? They've got the builders in.'

She laughs and squeezes his upper arm. 'Don't suggest I should sue them now! It was absolutely, entirely, my fault.'

Will says, returning the squeeze, 'I thought you said it was a long story!'

*　　*　　*

He wakes, in the dark, to the telephone ringing. He thinks, at once, of his father. He must be anxious to make his century and it would be typical of malicious chance to finish him off when the goal is in sight. He imagines Silas waking, shocking pain in his chest, ringing the desk. Night porters in old men's clubs must be used to emergencies, able to gauge more or less what action to take; ambulance service or private club doctor; telephone numbers of sons and daughters ready to hand.

This particular son will not be much use at the moment. It will be Coral who will have to rush to the club, to the hospital, make the funeral arrangements. There is an undertaker up the Essex Road, opposite the good fish shop and the good butcher: he sees it when he

142

is queuing for smoked salmon and fresh halibut on Saturday mornings. When he first noticed it, did he think of his father?

All this goes through his mind in perhaps fifteen seconds as he drags himself up to a sitting position and fumbles for the telephone on the night table. Careless of Coral not to move it to her side of the bed in the circumstances but she has had a lot of things on her plate, this hideous black eye for one, how the hell did she get it?

It is only at this moment, as he picks up the receiver, heart thumping, bracing himself to hear his father is dying, or dead, that he realises Carol must have been lying to him. A long story, indeed!

He says, hoarsely, 'William Mudd here,' switching on the lamp with his other hand, twisting round to look at his treacherous wife who is still sleeping soundly. Once Coral closes her eyes it takes an earthquake to wake her . . .

Alice says, 'Will, is that you?'

'Yes. Alice? D'you know what the time is? Where are you ringing from?'

'Hamburg. Of course I know what the time is in London. I assume that's what you are asking, not what the time is in Germany. For you it's just before seven o'clock in the morning, I always check when I make international calls, you know that. Sorry if it's early but I have to catch a plane and I assumed Coral would be awake, getting the child off to school. I thought you'd still be in hospital.'

'They threw me out yesterday. Coral usually sets the alarm for seven fifteen. Still pitch dark, of course, at this time of the year. I thought Father must have been taken ill, heart-attack, well, you know, at his age.'

'Is that so high on your wish list? No, sorry, of course it's not, such a thought would never enter your head. Are you okay now? I'm flying to Berlin today, I'm giving the keynote address, but the seminar I was going to chair has been cancelled, so I thought I might come on to London a day earlier. If it's a nuisance, I can find an hotel. I just thought . . .'

'No, of course stay with us.' Will glances at Coral who is stirring beside him. He says, more loudly, 'We're both looking forward to having you with us.'

Coral opens her eyes, yawning and stretching. Her damaged eye looks a fraction better than yesterday. How on earth did she do it? Was she mugged? Does she think he would be upset if she told him? He mouths at her, 'Alice,' and she raises her eyebrows.

Alice says, 'What are you giving him as a birthday present? I know he'll say he doesn't want anything but it'll upset him if there are no little parcels. Hannah says she's sure *that girl*, well, you know who she means, is bound to find the most perfect giftie. She's a bit obsessed, our older sibling. Do you ever see Madame?'

'Hannah?'

'Clare, you pinhead!'

'No, I don't. I thought you said Hannah was obsessed! At least she hasn't rung me up at an unearthly hour of the morning to ask if I know what my father's dead second wife's daughter is giving him for his birthday.'

'Hannah doesn't want to be upstaged, of course. But she also wants to please him. She minds more than you and I do.'

Beside Will, Coral is giggling silently. Will shakes his head at her.

Alice says, 'I don't mean that unkindly. You and I have other occupations. She's just got sheep. And her rheumatism won't let her look after them so she's handed them over to Julius. He's a saint, that man. But you mustn't be unfair to Hannah. It's not just the money, it's what it stands for. Concern, love, affection. Does he ever talk to you about what he intends to do with the rest of it?'

'No.'

'No? Well, he wouldn't, I suppose. I'd be prepared to bet that he does his best to stop any of my kids getting their paws on it. Not that I blame him for that. Did it ever occur to you, Will, that the three of us fulfilled what you might call normal parental expectations, me a scientist, you a publisher, Hannah a wife and mother, home-maker, whatever you like to call it, quite acceptable for a girl who grew up in the thirties, whereas none of our young, well, mine and Hannah's anyway, can't count yours, they're still being educated, have made much of a stab at real life? Even at paying their own way. My Georgy boy, he's the third one in case you've forgotten, has been coining a surprising amount making nose flutes out of old cigar cases, but I don't see it keeping him in bourgeois comfort exactly.'

'I thought you were in a hurry to catch a plane.'

'I've got a few moments. I don't often get a chance to talk to my baby brother.'

'Then I suppose it's more affluent times. Something like that? Take a year out after university. No one will starve if you don't get a job. Do your own thing. Have a baby at forty. Hannah's Jane gives up that good accountancy job because she wants a baby. Hannah says Jane says she *needs* to experience maternity. It's that word *need*. Children use it instead of *want*. But I don't think Father is interested in our children.'

'Not in his own, either.' Alice hoots with laughter. 'Nor in any *living* person. Ever occur to you, all the people his age he's known in his life are dead now? Friends, business acquaintances, their children too, a good many of them.'

'You can't know how he feels, all the same.'

'After Bella died, he came to stay with me. He wasn't so deaf then, more receptive, anyway. We talked quite a lot. I told him about

146

mice and tissue culture cells and he told me about tools, you know how boring he can be about tools, just as boring as me about mice, I dare say, but I realise now that nothing personal passed between us, not a word. Didn't matter, in fact it was rather pleasant, each of us talking about something we were interested in and not really expecting the other to listen, sharing a bottle of wine and looking at the lake before I went to collect the cooked lobster I'd ordered and he opened a second bottle. Then Jakey turned up. I'd told him to ring first but he didn't, and of course Father couldn't stand this hunk of young manhood sniffing round his daughter who ought to be past that sort of thing in his view. And that was the end of my lover.'

A pause. An echo over the line. Coral, getting out of bed and for the moment forgetting her injured eye, winks at Will. And then gasps with pain. Will screws up his forehead and thrusts out his lips, expressing his sympathy. Coral waves her hand, thanking him, telling him not to worry, and vanishes into the bathroom.

Alice says, in a quite different voice, 'I still find it quite hard to forgive Father for that. Jakey wasn't just a good fuck. I really did love that boy. And mother figure or not, I think he loved me.'

'I'm sorry.'

'Oh, well. Not Father's fault, really. Or not

directly. He was moderately discreet, just took himself off. But he put Jakey off me. Father made him take in how old *I* was, I suppose. Not very bright, Jakey, but he could just about manage to tot up the years. Maybe it was time we split, anyway. But there's been no one since. No one steady, that is. And I miss a nice bit of nooky.'

'I'm sorry,' Will repeats, feeling foolish. He has never before had this sort of confidence from either of his sisters. They have always been too old, for Christ's sake!

'Oh, don't be sorry!' Alice is sounding impatient. Looking at her watch, probably. She says, 'I should say sorry, running on. But I got diverted. What I really wanted to say was, don't worry too much over the birthday shenanigans. Or let Coral, either! Honestly, Will! I don't suppose he really wants this party, I'd be prepared to bet he's just going through with it because he thinks we expect it. Though I think none of us is very real to him any longer. He stopped feeling deeply about anyone else after Mother died. He was so caught up with her when she was no longer *there*, or not there in any real sense, that no one else mattered. Oh, except you, he didn't want *you* to know how ill she was, in what way. You were very *good* about that, at pretending. Hannah and I were very impressed! But to get back to Father, his feelings died with her. That's what I think.'

148

'What about Bella?'

'She was a convenience. For us too, of course. To be serious, although I dare say the sex was great for the age they both were, and I do think he was wonderfully comfortable with her, I don't think he loved her. Not as he loved Mother. Still—I'll say it for you—I can't know, can I? It's just speculation. And this call is costing a fortune. You know what hotel charges are like.'

Will wonders if he should say, 'Sorry I kept you,' but decides against it. Instead he repeats, with exemplary heartiness, how much he and Coral are looking forward to having Alice to stay with them, and puts the phone down.

The water has stopped running in the bathroom. Coral appears, wearing his towelling robe, and says, 'A long phone call for Alice. She's usually brisker.'

'She had time to kill before she had to leave for the airport. Alice doesn't like waste. Is your eye very painful?'

Coral shrugs. This is not worth answering. I am not worth answering, Will thinks resentfully. It occurs to him then, casually, without effort, as if he had opened a book in his mind, that Coral must have a lover.

He says, 'Everyone will think I've been beating you up.' And waits. But she has turned her back on him and is sliding the towelling robe from her shoulders. He watches her as she pulls on her clothes; her familiar

149

movements, her long, graceful back. She lifts her arms and her head disappears in her black sweater. She turns, pulling her hair free from the tight-fitting neck, lifting and twisting it. He says, 'You would tell me, wouldn't you?'

She sits on the dressing-stool to pin up her hair, smiling at him in the mirror. 'What, darling? What would I tell you?'

She looks so innocent. He cannot believe it. He smiles back at her. 'Oh, I don't know, my love. Everything. Nothing.'

CHAPTER ELEVEN

Silas is in aunt's small back living room talking to his father about the boy who was taken to Newcastle Infirmary in July 1930 with a steel ring stuck on his finger. The door is open on to the scullery to let in the light and the sun; Henry Mudd is sitting with his back to the curtained window and his face is in shadow.

Silas is saying, 'If you take two hammers of different weights and strike the one against the other, the lighter will spring further away. But if you have two hammers of exactly the same weight, they make an equal and opposite force. So when the boy's finger with the steel ring around it was laid on one fourteen-pound sledge-hammer and lightly struck with another fourteen-pounder, the ring, being brittle,

150

snapped at once without hurting the boy. I wish I could have explained this to you all those years ago when we first talked about it, but I didn't understand it myself until much later, when my friend Hans explained it to me. We were talking about jewellers, the tools they use for their work. You remember my friend Hans, from Denmark?'

Henry Mudd doesn't answer. Shades never do. Silas can attempt to expiate his own guilt but he cannot take the fear from his father's face, the fear that his son is mocking him for his foolish habit of regurgitating items of news that he reads in his newspaper. Punishing him. As if he is saying, 'Are you trying to impress me, you useless old man?'

*   *   *

And, of course, Henry Mudd doesn't know Hans from Denmark, though in a roundabout way it was through his faithful daily reading of the *Manchester Guardian* that Silas met Hans in the first place.

This was before Henry Mudd's stroke, before Alice was born; Effie and Hannah had gone to Edinburgh to visit her mother (the Writer to the Signet had died a year earlier, leaving Gladys Ogilvie a complaining widow) and Silas had driven from Norwich to spend Sunday with Aunt and his father.

'There was a piece in my paper,' Henry

151

Mudd said, 'not new, some months old now, but I cut it out when I got it because I thought it might interest you. Then we didn't see you for a bit and I forgot all about it. It only came to my mind the other day when I read about what they were doing in Germany, arresting the Communists. The piece I thought you'd like to see is about the swastika, you've heard of the swastika, it's the sign the National Socialist Party in Germany uses. It's also known as the Hooked Cross. No one knows who first thought of it, or what it was used for, but it came to Europe from Asia about the sixth century and was taken up by the anti-Semites as a symbol. Dramatic, you see, easily seen, and easier to draw than the hammer and sickle. Symbols can be powerful in politics. The Iron Front, that's the true German Socialist Party, democrats, liberals, thought up what seemed a good response to start with, three arrows painted across the swastika, cancelling it, making it harmless. But the Nazis struck back by turning the arrows into umbrellas, which made everyone laugh and cut the Iron Front down to size, made them look foolish. I can't remember exactly what happened after that. If you're interested, I'll try and find the cutting. Geneva is very good, she indulges me, letting me keep my old bits and pieces of newsprint. Of course, now most of the leaders of the Iron Front are either in prison or have left the country. I read the other day that the Nazis have set up a concentration camp for political prisoners in Dachau. Mostly Communists, I don't have much time for the Communists, but apparently there has been a lot of brutality and it doesn't look good for the future. I think we will have trouble with Hitler. What do you think, Silas?'

Henry Mudd rarely asked for an opinion on the news or comment he produced to entertain (or perhaps to propitiate) his son. If he asked what Silas thought about something, it was usually for form's sake; he seldom gave Silas time to reply. This time he waited.

Silas said, 'Oh, I wouldn't worry, Dad. Hitler's just a rabble-rouser when all's said and done. I think we can rely on the good sense of the German people.'

Aunt said, from the scullery, 'You're wrong, Silas.'

And later, after lunch, when Henry Mudd had fallen asleep in his chair and Silas was helping Aunt wash the dishes, 'Don't underestimate your father. He studies events, he reads history. Just because he's a bit old and sedentary is no reason to patronise him. You've done well for yourself and he's proud of you, but he struggles to understand what goes on in the world and you should give him credit for that. For my part if Henry tells me Hitler's a threat, not just to his own country but to the rest of Europe, I am more than ready to listen.'

For once, Silas had chosen to disagree with her. (Oh, how foolish he feels now, remembering!) He said, carefully wiping one of Aunt's best dinner plates, 'Did you see what Einstein said when he arrived in Antwerp the other day? He acknowledged that the situation for Jews in his country was dangerous just at the moment. But he also said he was convinced it was entirely a domestic matter, that the German government had no interest in starting a quarrel with the other nations of Europe. On the whole, Aunt, I think I would trust Professor Einstein to know what he's talking about.'

Aunt jerked her chin. 'I'd trust him to know the answer to a mathematical problem. But he can only speak of what he knows about Germany from a limited perspective. He's a Jew who's been living there and thanks be to God he's been able to get away, for all our sakes, not just for his own. But your father can take a broader and longer view. If he reckons there's another war coming, then I for one take it seriously. Your father's not a doer, Silas, I admit that, but he's quite a deep thinker. And he's put me in mind of what I must do. It will only be a bit, of course, but while I've got my health and strength I'll do my best to do it.'

*   *   *

154

It astonishes Silas now, looking back, how many useful people she knew. Or made it her business to know when she needed them. He knew, of course, that she had been a memorable teacher, and that many of the girls and boys she had taught called on her regularly, bringing their achievements to show her, their successes, their children, as they might once have brought her a bunch of hedgerow flowers picked on their way to school, but once he had left home, he had somehow not thought of her as continuing to live a wider life of her own. In fact, she knew almost every family in the town, from close friends, men and women she had grown up with, to the acquaintances she met at church every Sunday, or stopped to speak to in the market square. She chaired the committee of the Historical Association, arranging fortnightly meetings in Norwich and occasional lectures in the surrounding villages and towns. She bicycled energetically—the same old bike with the rusty skirt guard that Silas remembered from childhood—visiting neighbours, gossiping in the shops, keeping all her avenues open even in the difficult days of Henry Mudd's dying. One old friend, a distant relation of Coke of Norfolk and so carrying a certain clout socially, was ruthless in persuading friends and acquaintances that it was their duty to help finance Geneva Mudd's worthy project; Aunt herself was equally ruthless in finding school places and suitable homes in Norwich and the country around for 'her' children from Germany.

She had been unable to persuade Effie, though she had been tactful enough not to ask her directly. 'I think the poor things would be happier with their own kind,' Effie said to Silas. 'Besides, it's not fair on Hannah and Alice. They're the wrong age to cope with a stranger in the house. You know what Hannah is! She'd be *riven* with jealousy.'

'You could explain to Hannah, couldn't you? She's nearly nine years old, not a baby. Think about it, anyway.'

Silas, unwilling messenger between his aunt and his wife, realised uncomfortably that he was too nervous of them both to have formed any strong opinion of his own as to whether or not he and Effie should give a home to one of Aunt's refugees. Ashamed, he said, 'How would you feel if it were our little girls, Effie? Put on a train alone, leaving their mother and father behind and arriving in a strange country where they know no one, where most people don't even speak their language. Wouldn't you long to be told some kind family was going to take them into their home and take care of them?'

Effie widened her eyes, miming amused incredulity. 'But Silas darling, our children aren't Jewish,' she said.

Silas had done his best to justify Effie's

refusal to Aunt. 'She's worried about Hannah,' he said. 'Alice would cope all right, she's so sure of herself, always the brightest, top of the class, but Hannah's not nearly so confident. Effie thinks it would damage her to have to compete with someone who might take up too much of her mother's attention.'

Aunt had said nothing. Merely nodded and smiled and changed the subject. Did Silas know Hepzibah Pepys had passed away? Cancer, but mercifully quick; the poor old soul had only been bedridden for the last week or two. She was sure Arnold Pepys would appreciate it if Silas could spare the time to call on him to offer condolences. 'The funeral was last Wednesday,' Aunt said. 'I'd have let you know, and of course I put your name with mine on the wreath, but I knew you wouldn't want to interrupt your busy week, and I thought I'd spare you the trouble of thinking up good excuses.'

'I'm sorry, Aunt.'

The brightness of her eyes, the pert angle of her head, as she smiled up at him, said as plainly as words could have done that she knew what he was sorry about, and it wasn't having missed Hepzibah's funeral. He said, because he hated any falsity between them, 'I can't make Effie do what she doesn't want to do, Aunt. There's no arguing with her once she's made up her mind about something.'

'Or her mother has. She pays a lot of heed

to her mother, your Effie, not that I'd criticise her for that, it's too often the other way round with young women. But a good many people of her sort, Gladys Ogilvie's sort, of her high social class if you like, are not as shocked by what Hitler's up to as people like us think they ought to be. And Effie's young. Give her time, Silas, she'll come round to a right way of thinking, don't worry about it. Last thing I want to do is to make trouble between you.'

She had made trouble, all the same. Or trouble was already there for the making and she had merely given it a stir. Now, approaching his century, Silas settles on that conversation with Aunt (just before Hannah's ninth birthday) as a moment when his marriage was undermined by what he sees in his moments of anger as a kind of seismic shock; the plates moving, the earth quaking, changing the landscape for ever.

Over-dramatic, of course. (He knows that, he knows that; he knows it is the angry volcano erupting inside him.) He knows he loved, still loves, Effie. He would have sworn she loved him. All that had happened was that he had discovered he couldn't make her see what was going on in the world the same way he saw it. It was possible to disagree and still be happily married; it was just that he could no longer be happily married to Effie in the same way he had been. She had been perfection to him. On the rare occasions they had quarrelled, he had always apologised, never doubting that he was at fault. Now, when the shift took place and the ground shook beneath him, it was as if he had suddenly found, or been given, a new way of looking at her. Stubborn, limited, vain; a pampered young lady, spoilt and ruled by her mother.

It was painful to think that way and he had done his best to put it from him, telling himself that his wife had a perfect right to put her own children first. And that it was admirably honest of her not to pretend to humanitarian feelings she didn't possess. He couldn't be sure he possessed them himself for that matter. He was chiefly sorry that he had disappointed Aunt.

He did his best to make up for that disappointment with money, quite large sums, several hundred pounds at a time. This did not ease his guilt, merely tormented him further. He didn't want Effie to know what he'd done, he was too ashamed to ask Aunt not to mention it to her, and so lived in fear that she would. And then, when Aunt kept a discreet silence, he was further ashamed because it was clear she had understood without being told that the donations were to be kept a secret from Effie.

He felt sick with disloyalty. He had never hidden anything from Effie before. He dreaded her finding out. Why hadn't he told her? It was not that he couldn't afford it. The business was doing well. (He saw himself as a businessman now, not just an ironmonger who happened to own a number of shops.) And he and Effie had never quarrelled about money. Since she had always had enough, she was unworried by the possibility that she might find herself short of it sometime in the future. She wasn't particularly spendthrift, even if she spent more on her clothes than Aunt thought was proper in a young married woman with children to care for, saying to her face, 'Another new outfit, I see. I like to see you in your nice clothes, but I do worry about your cleaning bills. Baby's fingers are sticky.'

And once—only once—saying to Silas, 'She puts a lot of pound notes on her back, that girl of yours.'

She had overstepped the mark. Silas raised his eyebrows and she added, hastily, 'Well, why not? After all, you're not likely to land up in the workhouse and she won't be young and pretty for ever.'

He suspected that Aunt was taking advantage of the fact he had deceived Effie and was afraid she would find out. In fact, Aunt was blackmailing him, unconsciously perhaps, but effectively. It amused him to recognise that Aunt was jealous. It made him feel protective and even more anxious to please her.

*   *   *

'Hans Jensen,' she said. 'His name is Hans Jensen. Danish. A diplomat. The child is Ulrika Klemperer, she's the daughter of a friend of Mr Jensen's wife who is German though not Jewish herself, of course. Ulrika missed the *Kindertransport* so Hans offered to bring her. They should be arriving in London later this afternoon and he has to go back at once. I'm sorry to ask, Silas, such short notice and I know you're busy, but by the time I get to Norwich I'll be too late for the train . . .'

'It's all right, Aunt. Have you a place for her?'

'I'll take her for now. I'd prefer it if she could go into a family straight away, it's not the best thing for a girl to be stuck with an old woman, but there you are, it's all I can do in a hurry.'

The train was on time. He recognised Hans and Ulrika as they walked through the hissing steam up the platform, although he had no photograph, no description. He felt as if he had been waiting for them all his life. A slender, pale, anxious-looking man, wearing a dark coat buttoned to the neck, a stout little girl with firm rosy cheeks and dark curls, a red cape and red boots. A child in a fairy tale.

He went forward, hand outstretched. 'Mr Jensen? Silas Mudd.' The pale man looked at him doubtfully for an instant and then smiled, relief stripping years from his face. He spoke

English exactly and beautifully 'You have come to meet us? It is most good of you. Ulrika . . .'

He drew the child forward and she bobbed a curtsey, something Silas had never seen an English child do. Her brown eyes, fixed on his face, were round and wondering. She didn't seem frightened or bewildered as he had expected. He said, 'Hallo, Ulrika. Welcome to London,' and her eyes widened.

'I am afraid she cannot speak English,' Hans said. 'Only German, and a little French, I think. Ulrika, *parles-tu français*?'

She hid her face against his arm. He said, 'I am so sorry. She is only seven years old. I wish I could stay longer with her but I have to go back.'

He touched the child's head, pressing it into his side, and lowered his voice. 'Her parents were arrested two days ago in Vienna. They were waiting outside the British Consulate with many others. Several thousand, I think. They were all arrested and taken away. My wife had been visiting. She brought the child home with her. I was fortunate to be able to get her a visa.'

Ulrika pulled away from Hans Jensen and looked up at his face as if trying to read it. He spoke to her in German and she nodded and lifted her little chin. 'I have told her to be a good soldier,' Hans said. 'If you show her what you want her to do, she will do it. She is very brave and obedient.'

'My aunt has been learning German. I don't suppose she is fluent, exactly. But she will do her best for Ulrika. You can tell her parents . . .' He stopped. 'I'm sorry.'

Hans said, 'Do not apologise. What is happening is incomprehensible to a rational person. My train is not for a short while. Do you think we could sit down somewhere together? So Ulrika can become a little acquainted.'

They went to the tea room. Silas ordered tea and buttered scones. The child sat with her small leather suitcase on her lap, her arms locked across it. 'Shall we put it down?' Silas said, leaning forward to take it and gesturing at the floor beside her. She gasped and hugged the case closer. Her lower lip was thrust out.

'She won't be separated,' Hans said. 'She has carried the case like this all the time. I was not allowed to put it on the rack in the train. You can understand it, I think. It is all she has now.'

Appalled, Silas said, 'Tell her I'm sorry. Tell her that I won't take her case from her unless she asks me to carry it. No one will take it. Would she like an ice cream? She doesn't seem all that enthusiastic about the scones.'

Hans spoke to her and she shook her head. Her eyes had grown misty but she attempted a smile. Then she lifted her chin again and clung to her suitcase. Hans said, 'It is enough that you offer. It means you intend her no harm.'

163

The two men looked at each other. Hans said, 'Yes. It is terrible that a child should need to think like that. Do you have children?'

When he left, he shook hands with Ulrika. She stood very straight, her case in her right hand, watching him go. Then she gave her left hand to Silas. He couldn't see her face, only the top of her dark, curly head, her red boots. She said nothing in the taxi to Liverpool Street, nothing as they walked towards the platform where the Norwich train waited. He wondered if he should speak, what he should say, cursing himself for not speaking her language. He could try his unpractised French but that might only confuse her. If only she would look up at him, he could at least smile at her . . .

But she didn't look up. When they got into the first-class compartment she allowed him to lift her on to the seat but kept her eyes down, fixed on the suitcase she clutched on her lap. He said, because it seemed better to speak, even if she could not understand him, 'It's all right, Ulrika, everything's going to be all right, don't be afraid.'

She did look up then, solemn brown eyes on his face. And, perhaps reassured by what she saw there, the corners of her mouth twitched in a wary smile. Silas said, 'That's better. You'll be all right now. I have two little girls of my own. Hannah is older than you, but Alice is the same age.'

Whatever was he doing, taking Ulrika to stay with his elderly aunt instead of into his own home, with his own children? He wished he had thought to buy sweets for her. She had refused the ice cream but it would make him feel better to have something to offer her. If it had been his own daughters, they would be wailing for diversion already, kicking the seats, howling for something to stick in their greedy mouths. This child had such composure, such dignity.

He was startled to find himself seized by this sudden wave of anger against Hannah and Alice. He told himself he should be grateful that his children were safe at home. There were plans in this country, if war came, to disperse the population, evacuate young children and mothers with babies from the great cities into the countryside. Norwich was thought to be safe enough, but Effie had said if they lived in London or Birmingham she would never let her babies be sent away. She loved them too much, she said. Silas had accepted this as an unexceptionable sentiment, natural to a young mother, now he saw it as thoughtless and smug. In his mind, in the train, he argued with Effie indignantly. Did loving Hannah and Alice 'so much' mean she would rather they were blown to bits by a German bomb than separated from her? Did she really think Ulrika's parents didn't love their child because they had sent her to another country, to the uncertain comfort of strangers?

He wondered how much Ulrika understood, what was going on behind that creased little face, frowning out at the lit London suburbs racing past. He was relieved when she fell asleep, nodding over her suitcase, and hoped she wasn't dreaming.

Aunt was at the barrier, her face red, her eyes anxiously searching. When she saw them she held out her arms invitingly. Ulrika bobbed her stiff little curtsey and Aunt smiled. She said something in German, a hoarse, guttural sound to Silas's ears, a welcome presumably, and the child moved tentatively towards her. Aunt put her hands on the little girl's shoulders and looked down at her with her broad, loving smile. More German, several sentences—well rehearsed, Silas guessed.

And Ulrika laughed. Peal after peal of unaffected, clear, childish laughter. Aunt looked at Silas. Silas looked at Aunt. Other passengers, passing, turned and smiled. Ulrika spoke, hiccuping still with her laughter. Aunt bent to listen. Silas waited.

Aunt said, at last. 'I think she is saying I have an accent like a peasant,' she said.

*   *   *

Poor little girl, Silas thinks, all these years later, remembering how the painful colour flooded her face when she realised, as she had

166

almost immediately, that she had been impolite. It was beyond Aunt's linguistic skills to explain that she was not insulted; instead, she had laughed herself, heartily enough to persuade Ulrika that in this country to call someone a peasant was regarded as a great joke.

'It may make for difficulties later,' Aunt said, 'but we'll cross our bridges when we come to them.'

She had a car waiting; a friend to drive them home. When Ulrika realised Silas was not coming with them, her face crumpled—only momentarily, her guard was back before Aunt could notice. But she kept her eyes on his face, twisting round as the car drew away, until he was out of her sight. And his heart was wrung.

*   *   *

Other children fared worse. Silas knows that now, indeed, knew it long ago. Even before the first unbelievably terrible stories began to come out of Europe, he had listened to his aunt, to his father, to Hans Jensen, the Danish diplomat who became his friend. In the context of human suffering, Ulrika was lucky.

Her parents had been arrested in a wave of anti-Jewish demonstrations, wrecking of shops, burning of synagogues, in revenge for the shooting of a German diplomat by a young Polish Jew. This had happened in Paris.

Grynsban, the Jew, was seventeen years old. He had been refused a work permit and ordered to leave the country on the same day that his parents had been arrested in Germany and sent to Poland. He had gone out at once and bought a revolver. And so Ulrika's parents had been arrested outside the British Consulate in Vienna along with thousands of other Jews waiting for visas.

Silas does not know if Ulrika saw her parents again. She slipped out of his life as fortuitously as she entered it. A cousin of her mother's, an American doctor, turned up in England to claim her and take her home with him just after the outbreak of war. He rarely remembers her now, he does not know if she is still living, but when she does come into his mind, which is usually at the same time that he visits his father, she is always the same: an uncomplaining, heroic child, wholly admirable. And he softens inside, as he never does when he summons up his spoiled and demanding daughters as children. It is not (so he defends himself) that he is perverse, caring more for passing acquaintances than for his family. When he thinks of Will as a boy, his heart melts.

Which is strange, he tells himself, in the circumstances.

CHAPTER TWELVE

'Father?'

'Who's that?'

'Will, Father.'

'Who?'

'Your *son*, Father. Will. *William*, Father.'

'All right, all right, I heard you the first time. You all right, Will? Feeling better? Have a good night?'

'Yes, thank you, Father, much better. Did you sleep well?'

'Passable, passable. Coming to have lunch with me?'

'Afraid not. Sorry.'

'It's not raining, is it?'

'No. But I've still got this cough. And I've some work to catch up on. Manuscripts to read.'

'Oh, if you've got work to do. What's Coral up to?'

'If you want her to get you anything, she says she'll be glad to. Though she's going to collect Alice from Heathrow later on. Reason I rang, I thought I'd let you know they're repeating that series Coral was in a couple of years ago, *Magistrate*, it was called, a series based on a magistrates' court in Surrey I can't remember if you were in London. Coral was the woman on the bench who always took the side of the defendants. They're running the first episode on BBC One, this morning at twelve o'clock. Not exactly prime time but it's only an hour and you might like to fit it in before lunch.'

'I'll do that. Twelve o'clock. Midday. Thank you, Will. Anything else to tell me?'

'Don't think so, Father. Enjoy your breakfast. I didn't wake you up, did I?'

*　　　*　　　*

Will says, to Coral, 'I think I did wake him, in fact. Never know if it's better to ring him at this sort of time or later on, when he might have gone down to breakfast. It's a walk from the dining room to the telephone.'

'Besides, that telephone doesn't have a thingummy, does it? Microphone. Though I don't think he always uses the one he's got in the room. Can you switch it off?'

'I don't know how it works, I'm afraid . . . Darling?'

'Yes?'

'Is it really all right for me to stay in bed? You *really* don't mind lugging a tray upstairs?'

'It means I can eat my toast in peace.'

Coral, wearing jeans and a black woollen sweater, stands beside the bed smiling down at him. She has got thinner, Will judges. What is that a sign of? A love affair? Or a fatal illness? He asks himself, Which would you prefer it to

170

be?

'Why are you grinning like that? What's so funny?'

He says quickly, 'Just happy to be back in my own bed, in my own house, my own wife bringing me breakfast.'

'You do feel better, don't you?'

'Yes, I'm fine. I feel fine. A good deal finer than I did this time last week, anyway. What are we having for Alice's welcome supper?'

'I was going to ask you that. We've got various stuff in the freezer. A leg of lamb? Smoked salmon? Festive food. Or I can do some kind of spaghetti. And salad.'

'No, I'll cook. You're picking her up. Dinkie can lay the table. Have we got garlic for the lamb?'

'In the brown pot on the shelf to the right of the oven. I'll take the lamb and the smoked salmon out of the freezer now. Potatoes in the cellar, salad in the fridge. Anything else? Do you want me to peel the potatoes?'

Coral pulls a face, miming despair at the huge demands Will is making. He had said *he* would cook, hadn't he?

'No. No, of course not. I only wanted to know what we had in the house. It may have escaped your notice but I've been in hospital.'

Listening to himself, sounding so pathetic and petulant, Will is dismayed. Suddenly he hears the whole of this conversation with Coral as ringing with falsity; a cruel parody of the

171

foolish and jocular conversations long-married couples have with each other.

He says, helplessly, 'Sorry.'

Meaning that he is sorry to be such a bore, lying in bed, having to be waited on. And that he can understand why she has found herself a happier, healthier lover, even if he deplores it. Would he have done the same thing if she had been in his position, always something wrong with her, and he had been forced into being the attendant nurse, cook, secretary, child-minder, bottle-washer? Not that Coral has ever been ill, not really ill, not unless you count having babies and, as he remembers it, she made very little fuss about that. But if she had been a proper invalid? Imprisoned in hospital, leaving him free as a bird after he'd been for a husbandly visit, as *she* has been free all this last week?

How can he know what he would do? He has not, himself, been absolutely, totally faithful, but there have been only two occasions, both on sales conferences and both too long ago to be counted, he feels. Otherwise nothing more than velleities; distant, mooncalf yearnings. There was the nice girl in publicity with long, soft brown hair who, before she left to go to Random House, would often come to the wine bar with him at the end of the day. And the woman who ran the children's list when he launched his own small publishing house, now swallowed up and run by accountants. It was always lunch, in her case; she was married with children and had to go straight home in the evenings. And, thinking of older women, there was, of course, Bella . . .

But, surely, he would never have allowed himself to be drawn into a proper affair, a real-life commitment; secret meetings, telephoning from call boxes (Will has a mobile but Coral pays all the bills), weekends—though how weekends could be arranged he cannot imagine, unless Coral were to be mentally disordered and paralysed. And in that case, presumably, he would be taking care of Dinkie.

How has Coral managed it, for Christ's sake? How long has it been going on? *Who is the man?*

Coral is standing in front of her dressing-table now, peering into the glass, putting on makeup. Why is she bothering? Will plays with the idea of her lover being someone she is likely to meet at this early hour but can only come up with the newspaper boy or the postman, and recognises that both are unlikely: the boy is too young, the postman is always changing. She has always fussed with her face and her hair in the mornings, perhaps it has something to do with being an actor, always needing to be ready to present herself to the world as a shiny, desirable package.

'Why are you looking at me like that?' Coral

has turned from the looking-glass and is frowning at him.

'Like what?'

'Oh, I don't know, sort of accusing.'

'Good heavens! What on earth could I be accusing you of? Oh, I don't know, I'm just feeling fed up. I ought to be out of bed, getting on with life, I suppose I'm fairly fed up about that.'

'Don't take it out on me, then,' Coral says, not speaking angrily, but with a warning edge to her voice that is quite close to anger. Then, forcibly bright and determined, 'I think I'll make scrambled eggs. Quite easy to eat in bed. All you will need is a fork. Scrambled eggs and buttered toast in soldier's legs. That suit you?' And, turning at the door, 'I suppose my eye still looks hideous. I mean, that's what you were looking at?'

*   *   *

She has got into the habit of not really seeing the damage when she looks in the mirror. Now, in the kitchen, while the coffee machine hawks away on the counter like an old man with a blocked sinus, she examines her eye in the steamed-up glass over the sink. Not as bad as it was, but she still looks as if she has been in a drunken brawl and got the worst of it. Pity Will didn't warn Alice when she rang. The poor woman will be horrified when she

174

emerges from Customs at Heathrow. Perhaps she should dress up in Muslim gear to go to the airport, one of those beaky things over her nose and a black scarf round her head? Oh, perhaps not. She'll have to stick to the story about builders and paving stones; it gains veracity each time she tells it. Coral is beginning to believe it herself.

Believing your own fictions is a good way of dealing with real life, of course; turning raw terror into a digestible stew. Is she really afraid? She is a sensible, grown-up woman. Isn't she? What does she have to be afraid of? In the first shock, while she was on her own in the house, it was natural that she should hear sounds in the night, tremble when the telephone rang. But Will is home now, and Dinkie, and this evening Alice's arrival will more than complete the defence system: Alice on her own is capable of facing down any number of nameless monsters.

She could confide in Alice, who would laugh at her fears, blow them away; a crisp, fresh wind, clearing the skies. Though Alice might also laugh at Coral for entertaining the monsters in the first place; even suggest she is getting a kick out of it all; a sexual thrill out of the sense of danger. *Something is happening to me at last!*

But nothing is happening. Nothing happened since that horrible night. Coral has walked along the canal to the petrol station

175

where the young Asian had refused to let her into the shop, but had called her a taxi. She has walked past the apartment block but has seen no one either come in or go out. She knows she is a fool to go on these expeditions. She doesn't know why she is drawn to them. To try to go and meet what frightens her because it is easier than waiting for it to come to her?

He won't come to her. He doesn't know her name or where she lives. If he had found out somehow, and wanted to harm her, he would have shown himself already. On the other hand, although she may be safe at home, he lives near enough to share the same high street. Once outside the house there is always the possibility of a chance meeting: in the supermarket, the post office, the bank, the bus queue, the Angel underground station . . .

'Stop it,' she whispers, clenching her fists to her cheeks. '*Stop it.*'

And turns to the stove and begins to crack eggs into a bowl.

*   *   *

Will is woken by a bell ringing. Not the telephone this time, just a single peal. The front-door bell. Not the post, either: it is the afternoon, though daylight is fading. Almost four o'clock. Where is Coral? Oh, Christ, she's gone to Heathrow, to fetch Alice; Dinkie will be home from school in a minute; he should be doing something about food for this evening . . .

He is out of bed, shaky-legged, at the window. There is a taxi ticking in the road and someone on the pavement below him. A dark face is turned upwards. 'Special delivery.'

He calls out, weakly, 'Down in a minute.'

The cold air outside has started Will coughing. He closes the window and doubles up for a second, spitting into his handkerchief and inspecting the result: not exactly clear, but not too repulsively yellow either. He mutters, 'Cheated death again,' shuffles into his slippers and feels almost cheerful as he goes down the stairs, switching on lights, tying the cord of his dressing-gown. Maybe he'll be fit for the old man's birthday after all, even in good enough voice to recite the carefully judged speech he has already prepared— necessarily a bit of a gallop through such a long life, but flavoured with what he hopes are the right kind of jokes, sentiments and platitudes for the occasion. It is unlikely that Silas will be able to hear all he says, but Coral will tape it; she has already bought the tape and a Walkman as a present for Silas, so that he can play it over at full volume later. Typically thoughtful of Coral, Will reminds himself, and is conscious of a faint stir of guilt that is partly due to feeling that he should have thought of the tape himself, partly to shame at the way he has been suspecting Coral, excellent wife and excellent daughter-in-law,

177

of having a secret lover. It must be a hangover from his illness; from the toxic confusion, the strange, dream-like state that had induced him to see moving paintings on the yellow walls of his hospital room.

He opens the front door and a youngish, dark-skinned man in some kind of uniform— Will gets the fleeting impression of a dark, braided jacket—thrusts a bunch of flowers at him. 'Miss Mudd,' he says. 'Miss Coral Mudd?' And is back in the waiting taxi before Will can answer.

*   *   *

Alice says, 'You can understand Hannah. Well, I say that, though I can't honestly say that I do. But making a Herculean imaginative effort, it must be odd never to have made any money yourself, never to have collected a pay cheque, cash in hand, whatever. I suppose what you say of women like her is that they live through their husbands and children. Oh, I know Hannah's always done charitable work, but when you think about it, it's a bit pathetic that when they first moved out of Oxford to the back of beyond she told everyone she was going to be a shepherdess, as if she were giving herself an identity finally. Well, we know what happened to that notion. Poor Julius.'

Coral says, mildly, 'I think Julius enjoys looking after his sheep. People take hobby

178

farming seriously nowadays, don't they? Just as well with the real farmers doing so badly.'

'Always a man to make the best of things, Julius.' Looking out of the window at the crawling traffic in the Marylebone Road, Alice sighs. 'What a mess.'

Coral assumes she is referring to the choked arteries of the city rather than her brother-in-law's stoicism or her sister's marriage. 'Yes,' she says. 'Worse every day.'

Alice sighs again. 'You might not think it,' she says, 'but I dote on my children. Life's harder for them than it was for us in so many ways. Or so it seems to me. We were lucky, my generation, growing up before and during the war. We didn't have to *find ourselves*, the way mine are always saying they have to, there wasn't time, something more important was going on. Bigger than we were, you might say. And when it was over, things had to be put back together again. You felt, that is, I know I felt, there was something worth working for. For Hannah, it was always just Jane and Paul. They are her only achievements, and so it's enormously important to her that Father should take account of them. It's why she is so incensed about Clare and the money. Hannah's not greedy.'

'He's very old,' Coral suggests, braking suddenly as the lumbering truck in front decides, apparently on impulse, to turn left into Regent's Park. 'Maybe when you're as old

179

as that, you can't cope with too many people. If we were all dead, he might be keener to get to know his grandchildren.'

'Charitable of you,' Alice says, disapprovingly. 'He's always been one for strangers rather than his own.'

'Clare is very good. Rings him up, has lunch with him about once a week when he's in London. I think he is grateful.' Coral wonders why she is bothering to defend Silas who is quite capable of defending himself. She has no wish to be caught up in Hannah and Alice's hang-ups about their old father. Maybe she is just interested in keeping the record straight. She says, 'It's someone being *there* that matters. After all, Hannah's in Yorkshire, you're in Maine. And Hannah's children could go and see him. But they don't go. Nor do mine. In the vacations, that is, obviously they can't go in term time. I think they're both intimidated. I am sure Rory is . . .'

'I don't think Hannah's kids would be welcome, do you? Single mother. Gay dentist?'

Coral says, coldly, 'I don't think Silas is homophobic.' Though he might jib at a pregnant, unmarried granddaughter.

'Do you know something?' Alice is sounding surprised, as if something has only just struck her. 'I don't really know what he is or isn't. If someone asked me, "What's he *like*? What makes him tick?" I don't know what I would say.'

180

                    *   *   *

Will has put the huge bunch of yellow roses
into a big pottery jug and placed them on a low
table in front of the mirror that hangs between
the long windows of the first-floor drawing
room. The flowers, and their bright reflection,
light up the room on this grey day.

'How lovely.' Alice drops her small suitcase
(small enough to be hand luggage when flying)
and demonstrates her pleasure by putting her
hands together as if in prayer. 'What a lovely
welcome, Will. What beautiful flowers.'

'I didn't buy them. I mean, I would have
bought flowers for you, Alice, but Coral told
me to stay indoors. The roses were sent to her,
I suppose by an admirer.' Afraid he is
sounding as grim as he feels, Will smiles—he
fears like a maniac. 'A secret admirer, that is.
No name attached. Maybe Coral will know.
They showed a rerun of one of her
programmes today, it's possible that someone
found out where to send flowers from
someone or other. I don't think her agent
would give her address, but you never know.
Someone new in the office . . .'

The front door bangs. Coral has returned
from parking the car. Will can hear the tinkle
as she drops her keys into the dish on the hall
stand, her step on the stair. Will finds he is
trembling. He is still smiling, his fierce, mad

smile. As Coral comes into the room he waves his hands at the roses in a grand, theatrical gesture and says, 'Behold! Lovely surprise. These came for you. An unknown admirer!'

And to his distress, to his terrible pain, Coral looks horrified. The crimson colour floods her neck, her face. Turning away to hide her confusion she mumbles 'I don't know. I simply cannot imagine . . .'

CHAPTER THIRTEEN

Silas cannot be certain when Effie first lied to him. At the time it would have been inconceivable to him that she could lie to anyone. Later, looking back, he fixed on one summer evening, a Friday, 1943 probably, though after more than half a century he cannot be certain, those grey years of war merging in his mind into one long chronicle of wasted time. Time without Effie.

He was now at the Ministry of Supply, which had taken over the Ministry of Aircraft Production where he had started his war work, and was living in the basement of a bombed house in Belgravia, occupying the only two rooms that remained habitable. He had tried to persuade Effie to take the girls west, Shropshire or Wales, safer than East Anglia once the Germans had occupied the Low

182

Countries, but she had said they were safe enough where they were, she could visit him in London, he could come to Norwich.

'I couldn't bear for us to be torn further apart than we have to be, darling. At least as things are, I can see you, be able to *touch* you at least once a week.'

Her sweetness enraptured him. He loved her then as he had loved her in the beginning, emotionally, physically. Alone in his creaking basement in London, he ached for her; travelling home at weekends in the crowded wartime train, his pulse raced with excitement and longing. And yet, as soon as he walked through the door, he felt awkward and stilted, shy as a boy. It bewildered him. He knew he had never been garrulous, but this strange stiffness was new, he couldn't account for it. He could see that it puzzled her. She would say, 'Are you all right, darling?'

And on this particular evening, she turned away from his kiss and said, 'You don't have to come home every weekend, you know. If you've got something better to do.'

For a moment he was shocked into silence. Then he said, 'Don't you want me to come?'

It was the wrong thing to say, he knew that as soon as he'd spoken. He should have told her how he felt, how much he missed her, how he was seized with strange fears, half afraid as he walked from the station that the house would be empty when he got there, that she would have mysteriously vanished. Or that she had never been, that it had all been an illusion, his love for her, his life with her. And then, when he knew it was not and she was running to meet him, he was speechless with joy. As he was speechless now.

She shrugged her shoulders. 'Up to you, isn't it?'

He gazed at her helplessly.

She said, 'You don't seem all that pleased to be here.' The angry colour rose in her cheeks. 'You don't have to come for *my* sake. I've got more than enough to do, I'm not just sitting here, waiting.'

He thought he understood. He said tenderly, 'Oh, my love, you're unwell. I'm so sorry, I should have remembered. You ought to be resting.'

'*God!*' she shouted. 'Christ. I am not, I repeat, *not*, getting my period!'

And she rushed from the room, ran upstairs. The bedroom door slammed. Hannah, hefty in her school-uniform gingham, emerged cautiously from the dining room where, so Silas assumed from the ink on her cheek, she had been doing her homework. She said, with a conspiratorial grin, 'What have you done? What's wrong with Mother?'

'I don't know' He attempted to smile. 'It's nothing for you to worry about anyway. How are you, Hannah? Have you had a good week at school?'

'Average bloody,' she said. 'No more, no less. You know I hate school. You must have said something to Mother to make her fly off the handle. Though she's been pretty bloody all week.'

'Don't use that word, Hannah. Please.'

'Why not? *She* does, all the time. All right, she's been in a state. Hell to live with. Exhausted is what she calls it. Out every night working down at the Churchill Club for American Officers. Poor lonely boys, she says, far from home. And I have to babysit if you want to know. Get its breakfast, see it's got its milk money in its pocket, see it cleans its teeth and washes behind its ears.'

From upstairs, Alice called, 'Hannah. *Hannah!* Who are you talking to?'

'Who'd you think, stupid? Father, of course. The old fool's come home to make trouble as usual.'

The child—horrible child but still *only* a child, Silas reminded himself—regarded him with what he could only describe as triumphant malevolence. He said, as equably as he could manage, 'If Aunt Geneva were still alive, she would tell you to wipe out your mouth with soap. I am telling you to go back to the dining room and finish your homework and when you have finished it, not before, come out in a better frame of mind. Your mother is doing her bit for the war effort, I can't see it hurts you to look after your sister.'

185

'War work! Is that what she says it is? It's not what I call it.'

'Hannah! That is quite enough.'

He thought, *I could hit her!* He did in fact take a step towards her and only stopped himself raising his hand with an effort. He said, 'Go to that room now, this minute, and stay there. I don't want to see you again today.'

She was red as cooked beetroot. She said, 'I haven't had any supper.'

He looked at her, deliberately allowing his eyes to travel up and down her body. He said, 'Going without food for once won't do you much harm. In fact quite the opposite, I would say.'

And he marched down the hall and up the stairs without another glance at his older daughter, righteously indignant but grateful, all the same, for Alice's timely appearance on the landing above him, ready for bed in her pyjamas. He bent to kiss her and said, in a loud, cheerful voice, 'Well, I hope you're pleased to see me, young Alice. I could do with a bit of a welcome.'

Alice looked up at him with her usual serious expression, but then she put her arms round his waist and squeezed him tight.

She said, 'My rabbit's had babies. I haven't counted them because I didn't want to disturb her in case she decided to eat them, but I think we could go and look at them now, if you like.'

*   *   *

Effie was lying on the bed, on her back, staring at the ceiling. Silas said, 'I'm sorry.'

'What for? You haven't done anything. I'm the one should be sorry. I've been horrible to you.'

'I wouldn't say that was your fault. I freeze up. I can't explain why, but I can see it might seem unfriendly.'

'I didn't mean just now' She moved her head restlessly. 'I mean, in general. When you're not here. Going out, enjoying myself. Drinking too much occasionally.'

'That doesn't sound likely. You're not—'

'Oh, not getting *drunk*. just enough to make things more bearable. And to be friendly. Some of the boys are all right, those who've found a local girl mostly, but the others are lonely. It's not an easy job, Silas. I don't just pour the drinks!'

'What else do you do?' He smiled.

'Oh, you know! I flirt a bit, just enough to make some of them feel a bit better. Only it makes me feel guilty.'

'Why should it? Unless you do more than flirt.'

He looked at her. Her eyes were still fixed on the ceiling. He said, 'You don't, do you? Do more than flirt, I mean.'

She looked at him then. She said flatly, 'You ought to know me better than that, Silas.'

He sat on the bed. 'What's wrong with Hannah?'

'Growing up. Adolescent. She resents my not being here all the time, attending to her every need. No, that's unfair. I give Alice her tea before I go off but Hannah won't eat with her. She says she's old enough to have a proper dinner in the evening. I don't know what she imagines. Seven courses and footmen in white gloves.'

'Do you have to go to the club every night?'

'No. No, I don't.' She sat upright; hostile, accusing. 'I enjoy it, Silas, if you want to know. It's not all duty, though it is sometimes. I need a bit of fun in my life. Have you any idea what it's like for me, stuck here with the girls, day in, day out, no one to *talk* to, not even a woman to help in the house. Then you come back . . .'

Her face crumpled suddenly. 'I didn't think it would turn out like this.'

He put his arm round her shoulders, cradling her. He said, making a joke of it, 'Well, you know there's a war on.'

'That's not my fault, is it?' she wailed. 'I didn't start it.'

He wanted to laugh. But then he saw her resentment was real, not just a momentary descent into childishness and it chilled him. He said, 'You opting out, then? I dare say a lot of people would like to know how to do that.'

She was crying now, sadly and silently, tears

spilling, and he felt a distant pity. It wasn't Effie's fault that life had always been made easy for her; it was natural that her expectations should be pleasant ones. And no use, he knew from experience, to try to point out to her that, compared with most wives in wartime, her situation was not so disagreeable. She had her own familiar roof over her head, her children with her all the time and her husband at weekends. No Lily—but surely no sane, healthy woman would wish to take another out of the armed services or the munitions factory to clean her kitchen floor? He dismissed the small, half-amused voice that said Effie would be only too happy to deprive the war effort for her own greater comfort, and put himself to the task of making the weekend bearable for her without the excitement of the Officers' Club.

He said, 'We could go out to eat, if you like.'

She gave a last, dying sob. 'It's not fair to Hannah. I promised her she could have supper with us. And you know what she is.'

'Just at the moment I'm not sure that I care,' he said grimly.

*   *   *

You ought to know me better than that. Well, he did know her better, even if he had been unable to admit it to himself then. When he did admit it, he understood that Effie had

189

been as honest with him as it was in her to be. She had expected him to understand she was sleeping around, and not only to accept it without argument, in silence, but to forgive her on the grounds that her motives were purely quixotic; comforting the foreign soldiery was her patriotic duty. Perhaps she had assumed she had, if not his consent, at least his unspoken acceptance. Perhaps she thought he was unfaithful too, those lonely weeks at the Ministry, tit for tat, less said the better.

When he realised this, when he could no longer escape it, he was amazed that he had not seen the truth clearly before. He searched for explanations. He was naturally monogamous and she was not. It had never occurred to him that she might sleep with another man, because he had never considered making love to another woman. Effie was enough for him. He loved her more than she loved him. Or her love, being more open and generous, could embrace other people.

He decided, to his chagrin, that he had been too caught up in his anger with Hannah that summer evening to take in what her mother had been trying to tell him. He had heard what Effie said, and recorded the words, but it was as if he had only been listening with his ears, not with his emotions. He couldn't blame Hannah, not in justice or logic, but for quite a long time it made him dislike her. He shrivelled inwardly when she came into a room, her voice grated on him, he could see nothing admirable in her; she was neither clever like Alice, nor beautiful like her mother, nor good, as Aunt had been.

He was deeply ashamed. He knew he was wrong. A man should not feel repelled by his teenage daughter. He fought against it. He forced himself to smile at her, to kiss her, morning and evening, to ask about her school lessons, her friends.

He struggled to love her. He believed he had put up a good enough show to convince her. When he took both girls out in London on VE night, she clung to his arm with confident affection, trusting him to protect her from the rejoicing and boisterous crowd. She was looking excited and unusually pretty, her round face flushed and healthy, her eyes clear and shining. When the singing began, he heard her voice soaring, bell-like and true. He said— shouted—into her ear, 'I didn't know you could sing so well, Hannah,' and she smiled at him proudly. 'Mother says I am to have lessons now the war is over. I don't want to read music at university, I want to read modern languages, but I want to sing as well.'

He was pleased with her for the moment. He said, 'I may buy that house where I'm living now. The lease, that is. I've been thinking we might move down from Norfolk and live there. Good for all of us. There will be a better choice of music teachers in London.'

Alice, hanging on to his other arm, said, 'Mother won't like that. Leaving Norwich.'

He hadn't spoken to Effie about living in London. But this wild, happy night seemed to throw open doors to the future. Anything and everything was possible. He said, 'Won't she, Alice? Why not?'

Alice said, 'Hannah knows why.'

'Hannah?'

Hannah turned her face away. He could only see the curve of her cheek. She said, 'Don't pay any attention to Alice. She doesn't understand anything.'

Alice said, 'Oh, yes, I do. Don't patronise me, Hannah.' And she twisted away from Silas and would have bolted if he had not seized hold of her, locking his hand around the soft flesh of her upper arm till she squealed.

'Sorry. But if you ran away on a night like tonight, we might never find you again.' He wondered, briefly, if sons would have been easier to bring up than daughters. He said, 'Forget I said anything. I shouldn't have mentioned it before I had spoken to Mother. Of course it'll be her decision. But it's a beautiful house, or will be once it's rebuilt, and she will enjoy the shops and the theatres . . .'

He was conscious of all the people around them, pushing and swaying, laughing and crying, clutching each other, and of Hannah, seventeen, glowing and rounded: an obvious target for all the young men who had not yet

192

found a girl to cling to and kiss. He said, 'I think you've both had enough celebration. You've cheered Mr Churchill, you've been to the Palace, I'm tired if you're not.'

He put an arm firmly round Hannah's waist and kept tight hold of Alice's hand. He wished Effie were with them; without her he felt old and rejected, a middle-aged man with no function in this screaming and sweating crowd except to protect two young females from being kissed by a soldier. He envied the uniforms: to be entitled to wear one might have saved him from this sudden and desperate feeling that the war had rolled over him, taking his youth and his energy, and left him at the end of it, stranded in the Mall, with an aching back and sore feet and two tiresome daughters.

He said, 'Time to go now.'

*   *   *

Silas cannot remember now whether it was the next morning or the following one that the letter came. The girls were still with him, camping out in the basement of the bombed house, playing at being housewives, busy getting breakfast, when he heard it flop through the letter-box on the floor above the kitchen, on to the cracked marble floor of the hall. He went up the dusty, uncarpeted stair, which he only used when the post came; the front door had been sealed up after the bomb fell and the only way to get to the street from the basement was through the area door.

It was an old, re-used envelope. He recognised Effie's handwriting as he bent to pick it up and wondered why she had written; there was no telephone in the basement, but he always rang her in the morning, either from the Ministry or from the office in Covent Garden, which he had bought from a small publishing company when it moved offices to the country early on in the war. In fact, she must have spoken to him at least once, and possibly twice, after she had written and posted this letter. Was it an anniversary of an occasion he had forgotten? Or simply that she wanted to write to him? A love letter . . .

Effie's writing was large, with well-rounded letters and flourishing capitals. In spite of his familiarity with her ornamental style, Silas did not find the letter easy to read. Disbelief was a factor; he found that he had to read the first page several times before he comprehended what she was telling him. And he still could not believe it. It was a monstrous game. A cruel joke. She had been kidnapped and some lunatic had stood over her with a knife, or a loaded gun, forcing her to write these absurd lies to her husband who loved her.

It couldn't be true. It *wasn't* true. Ludicrously, in the end, she said that she loved him. She signed herself, 'Your sad, bad, but still loving little wife.'

He tore the letter up. The staircase that led to the first floor was unsafe to use, the banister broken and dangling, and there were wide openings in some of the risers. He pushed the shredded paper into one of these cracks scratching his hands so savagely that the blood ran. Then he sat on the bottom stair, sucking his lacerated fingers, gathering his courage to go down to his daughters, innocently making toast in the kitchen.

*   *   *

Eighteen months years later, when the builders began work, he lurked in the hall as they demolished the useless staircase, seized by what he realised was a foolish fear that the letter might still be legible if an inquisitive workman were to fit the pieces together. But when the staircase collapsed, making oddly little noise, not much more than the suspiration of exhausted timbers, a groan, or heavy sigh, it was into a pile of indiscriminate dust and rubble and Silas retreated, coughing, to the street, both relieved and frustrated: at the back of his mind, so peripheral he had barely acknowledged it, had been the thought that he just might rescue enough fragments to read the letter again, check what she had actually written against his faulty memory.

Now, in his great old age, he regrets the loss

even more. When he sits in the club library after breakfast, his father's favourite newspaper (which is no longer published in Manchester) draped over his lap, eyes half closed, doing what he calls *going over his life,* he can see Effie's opulent handwriting with his mind's eye, but apart from her last, lying farewell, her false declaration of love, he can only summon up an isolated word or phrase from that hypocritical letter.

If he had it now, in his hand, he would read it with pleasure, partly out of straightforward curiosity, but chiefly because it would set him off on one of the agreeable spurts of anger that are among the few sensations nowadays that make him feel fully alive. There are some sentences that he is sure appeared somewhere in the course of Effie's torrent of self justification. He runs them through, savouring their flavour. *The man I was born for. This thing is bigger than both of us. A love like nothing I could ever have imagined.*

And so on. The stupid, shallow, cheating bitch. He feels warmer already. He is not in the least ashamed of using Effie to get his blood flowing again this cold morning. It can't hurt anyone. It is entirely between the two of them, anyway. And she is dead.

What was the man's name? Something McDermot. American. Not his given name, the nickname Effie would have murmured so tenderly, it drives him wild with rage now he thinks of it. It will come to him in a minute. She had been carrying on with him for a year. That wasn't how she put it in her letter, of course. They had *come together.* He was *the love of her life.* Naturally. Not in Effie's nature to admit to enjoying a fuck. But she did, oh, she did! Oversexed, that was *her* nature. That was what they said about the Americans, too. Over-paid, over-sexed, and over-here. Silas supposes he was lucky she hadn't accused him of letting her down in that area. Complained about his performance, as she might well have done if she was contrasting his middle-aged, husbandly efforts with the lustier gymnastics of the younger American soldiers of which there had been several before the love of her life turned up on the scene. Not that she had ever seemed disappointed, he has to admit that. Which made it all the harder when she made it clear that McDermot was worth more to her not only than he was, but more than their whole life together, their home, their daughters . . .

That shit, McDermot. McDermot, McDermot—*Dolly*, that was the ridiculous name he went by. If he wasn't feeling all at once so agreeably sleepy, Silas could work up a good healthy fury, get himself going well enough to go for a short walk before lunch. Not that he enjoys walking any longer, London pavements being so wretchedly uneven, but it means he gets up an appetite for a good meal, double gin-and-It beforehand, a half-bottle of decent claret.

He composes himself for a short sleep, twenty minutes is what he allows himself in the mornings, and his body timer is efficient at delivering the correct waking moment. He checks the time by his watch. Twenty minutes will bring him to eleven forty-five. A prophylactic trip to the lavatory and he will be ready for his constitutional. 'Dolly,' he mutters. 'Dolly McDermot . . .'

*   *   *

Will comes out of the shower, trips over his big towel as he hurries out of the bathroom, trips over the edge of the carpet as he runs to answer the ringing telephone.

His father's voice, a bit croaky 'Will? Will? That you? Didn't wake you up, did I?'

'No. No, of course not. I've been up for hours. You all right, Father? Getting geared up for the party tomorrow? Alice was wondering if you were too busy for lunch today. She though she might drop into the club. Only if you're free, of course.'

'What? Yes, yes, speak to her in a minute. One thing at a time. Did Molly get the flowers yesterday?'

'Molly? Flowers . . .?'

For a second Will cannot remember who Molly is. Then he remembers. His father's long-dead sister. His long-dead, never-known aunt. But flowers? Oh. Of course. Molly the actress.

He finds himself laughing. Amazement. Relief. He says, 'Yes, Father. Flowers came for Coral. That is, I think you meant them for Coral, didn't you?'

'What's that? I'm not picking you up.'

'Yes. Yes, Father. Coral got your flowers. Lovely flowers. She was delighted.' He looks at himself in the mirror that hangs behind the table in the hall where the telephone stands, the family diary that Coral keeps up to date and open so the whole week can be seen at a glance, and sees himself grinning away like an idiot. Well, he is an idiot. A suspicious fool. He says, 'I am delighted, too. Thank you.'

'I forgot to put a card in. Just tell her I thought she was very good in that television thing. Took me a bit of time to work out which one she was, but pass it on, will you? My compliments. And I will have a word with Alice. She around? Put her on, will you? Are you listening, Will? Have I said something funny?'

'No, Father. Sorry, Father. You said just the right thing. Cheered up the morning. The flowers were really beautiful. I'm so glad you remembered. Hang on. I'll fetch Alice.'

CHAPTER FOURTEEN

'God,' Alice says. 'I could sleep for ever. Still, midday's better than nothing. Daft of you to suggest I have lunch with him. I need to wash my hair, tidy myself before I can face the sharp paternal eye. He's got more sense than you have. He said tomorrow at the party would be quite time enough for us to meet. Not exactly flattering to me but certainly convenient. Coffee?'

'Burping away. Can't you hear it? The machine needs rodding through, whatever you call it. It's one of the things I'm supposed to do and I never remember. You look well, Alice.'

'That's what people say when you've got too old to be told you look beautiful. You don't look too bad yourself, in spite of apparently failing health. I suppose a decently serious illness every now and again gives you the chance to lie up a bit. In fact, you look both well and handsome, little brother. If you think that sounds too fulsome, I'll qualify it. You look better than you looked last night.'

'Do I? Oh, well. Get to my age, one's a bit up and down.'

'What age? You're a child. I don't expect you and I to have an Organ Recital. That's what Hannah calls the kind of conversation old people have with each other.'

Will says, 'When Disraeli found he was forgetting the names of fellow members of the House of Lords, he put his arm round their shoulders instead, and said, "How's the old disease?"'

They both laugh. Will pours coffee for Alice, sitting at the kitchen table in her cotton wrapper, and thinks, with pleased surprise, that he likes her better than he used to. She has always been his preferred sister but what he feels for her at this moment is a more positive warmth than he remembers feeling before. It is not just that she is looking so pretty, flushed and rested after her long sleep. Perhaps as they have both grown older the age gap between them has dwindled. He is no longer a child to her, she is no longer an adult to him. They are equals now, and so different people to each other. *His* Alice is the Alice he knew when he was a child, four or five, and she was a young woman, running beside him as he learned to ride his first bicycle. Now she is in her sixties and, suddenly, an interesting stranger to him. What is Hannah's Alice like? Father's Alice? The Alice known to her children? To her scientific colleagues? To her young, departed lover?

Alice says, 'You'd think Julius could *do* something about Hannah, wouldn't you? A clever man like him. That's not really a question, I know the answer. Being clever doesn't help you to see what's going on with someone close to you. She ought to see a doctor. A therapist. They're just coming down by train for the lunch and going home straight away afterwards. She gets nervous if she's away from home for the night, Julius says. That was last night when I spoke to him. And he said had you remembered when you were doing the seating plan that she had to be able to escape. She mustn't be trapped against a wall. I said you'd told me it was a big oval table in the middle of the room so there was no difficulty. Then I spoke to Hannah and she asked after Coral's eye. I said she *said* she'd fallen over on the pavement but that was a likely story and it was my opinion our saintly baby brother had bashed her up.' She gives an unexpectedly girlish giggle.

'Unwise,' Will says gloomily. 'She'll brood and ponder and start to believe it.'

'It'll give her an interest. One thing does puzzle me, though. You'd have thought Coral would have put out her hands to save herself. But last night at dinner—you can't help looking at Coral's hands, they're so disgustingly, enviably elegant, those lovely long, white fingers—I couldn't see a single scratch, not even a broken nail.'

'Wearing gloves? Thick gloves, we're having a cold winter.'

'I suppose so. Though I'd have thought her hands would have been bruised anyway. And if she hadn't used them to break her fall, she

202

would have more general abrasions, wouldn't she? Cheeks, chin, forehead. But no. Smooth as alabaster.'

Alice has always prided herself on her powers of observation, Will remembers. A harmless amusement most of the time; just now, unfortunately, this is a matter on which Will is vulnerable. He snaps at the sister he was regarding with favour only a few moments ago. 'What are you suggesting? What devious game do you think poor Coral is playing?'

He repents immediately. Alice enjoys being an amateur detective. If she were not a world-famous scientist, she might have written charming detective stories featuring a small female sleuth, either amateur or professional but certainly with scientific interests, and made a great deal more money. He says, changing his tone to one of calm, brotherly interest, 'What are you working on at the moment?'

Alice smiles kindly. 'The same thing I have been working on for years, Will darling. We study the minor transplantation antigen genes in mice, because although they may not have an exact human counterpart, there is a set of transplantation genes on the Y chromosomes that are almost identical in mice and humans. If we can find out the precise molecular identity of these genes, we may be able to get to grips with some of the complications in bonemarrow transplant patients. And in fact, perhaps I should *whisper* it, we are more or less *there.*'

She stops, looks at him a little sadly, and pulls a wry face. 'Sorry, but you did ask. It probably means more to you if I say we may be able to help the treatment of cancer. Bone-marrow transplantation can be used as therapy for people with leukaemia, for example. But there's a disease called GVHD, that's graft-versus-host disease, when the alien bone marrow turns on the host, destroying the skin, the liver, the whole bloody works. The immune response to grafted tissue is controlled by cell surface proteins called histocompatibility antigens—sorry about that but it's what they're called. Had enough?'

Will shakes his head. He is fascinated, awed, indeed, not so much by what she is telling him, but by the way it seems to change her, from his middle-aged sister to a mysterious figure who is out of his depth and his reach, a god who speaks an arcane and loftier language that he, a mortal, will never be able to master.

He says, 'Professor Mudd. Honoured Professor. You make me feel like an illiterate savage.'

She frowns. 'I wish I could explain it more clearly. It's not really so difficult. You can cut down on the risk of rejection by matching the donor and the recipient for the six major histocompatibility antigens, but you get problems if there is a mismatch with the minor antigens. We want to clone the genes for a particular sub-set of these antigens. That's what I'm doing, Will. I think it's the first time you've asked me about it.'

'I'm sorry.'

'Don't be. It's the language. Double Dutch. Chinese. I think I understand how you publish books but I expect if you started to explain all the technical stuff, I'd be lost in a minute. Likewise acting. I can stand on a stage and give a lecture, but if I was asked to pretend to be someone else, I would fall apart. Collapse in split seconds. It's really lousy luck about Gertrude.' The girlish giggle again. 'For Coral, I mean. She's being gallant about it but she's obviously upset and I assume that's why. Unless . . .?'

'No,' Will says. 'No. There's nothing else to worry her, far as I know.'

*　　　*　　　*

Coral is having her hair fixed for the birthday lunch, an operation that entails sitting under a strong light and facing a large, clear looking-glass that does her no favours. Before she left home she had checked in the mirror behind the telephone table and thought the eye seemed marginally better. Another night's rest and careful theatrical makeup, and she might pass for human. Above all, she didn't want the old man to notice. It might not spoil his day but it would make hers more uncomfortable, having to listen to his ripe comments on her misfortune in his deaf man's loud voice.

She tells herself, If that's all you've got to worry about then you're laughing! She hears her voice speaking this line in the accent she had adopted for her role as the coarse-tongued but gallant and cheerful pensioner in that last, long-running soap; moderately genteel Essex with a faint Cockney echo. How would that indomitable heroine have coped with a lunatic stalker? 'Straight to the police, my duck, PDQ, no problem.' And say what? 'I got into his car and hurt my face when he braked too hard. I thought he didn't know where I lived, but he's sent me a bunch of beautiful roses . . .'

Who else could it be? Oh, people, admirers, have sent her flowers before, and sometimes, if only very occasionally, anonymously. But in the circumstances such a coincidence is surely unlikely. He had seen the episode of *Magistrate*, by chance presumably, found her name in the newspaper, or the *Radio Times*, and looked up her address in the telephone book. Her agent advised his actor clients to go ex-directory, especially if they were female and appearing in long-running shows, but Will had objected: Coral didn't live alone, she had him to protect her. He also believed—although he didn't put this forward as an argument, Coral knew how he felt about it—that removing one's number from the telephone book was a shameful sign of self-importance.

The roses might simply be an apology. But why not attach a name in that case, a brief letter? Unless, realising she was an actor, he feared she might sue him for damages?

Then why send the roses at all?

'Very nice,' she says, smiling at Gemma, the older stylist who always does her hair so well and without too much chat. Though a bit of chat might have eased her mind this morning, or at least provided a temporary diversion. She says, 'I'm not working at the moment, can't do anything until my eye is better, but I wanted my hair done for my old father-in-law's hundredth birthday tomorrow. Can you imagine being that age? I don't suppose I'll reach it. Lousy genes. I don't come from the right kind of long-lived family.'

Gemma produces a hand mirror and holds it so that Coral can see the back of her head. She says, 'You should count yourself lucky, Coral. My grandmother will be a hundred and three next Sunday. She says all the years since she celebrated her century have been nothing but anticlimax. She's bored rigid. Mind you, she's always been a bit of a moaner.'

They smile at each other. They are much the same age. Gemma has been doing Coral's hair for the last twenty years. Whenever Coral has been resting, that is. At one time they had both thought Coral might one day become so famous that Gemma would become her personal beautician and hairdresser, travelling with her when she was filming on location, attending her at the theatre, but they have never mentioned this ambition to each other and it has faded gently at about the same rate from both their minds, only mildly regretted, without serious pain.

'I hope your eye gets better soon,' Gemma says. 'It's not too bad, really. I dare say it looks worse to you than to other people. You've got such lovely bones and beautiful eyes, that's what people see when they look at you, not a temporary blemish.'

She says this not as flattery but as a sincere old friend making a considered judgement. Coral wishes now she had told Gemma how she had damaged her eye. Too late now, too long a story when she is just leaving, she should have spoken earlier. *I did what our mothers always told us we shouldn't do, and accepted a lift from a stranger. He turned out distinctly weird and I got scared—foolishly I expect, he was probably perfectly harmless. Then he braked suddenly and I went into the windscreen and I worked myself up into what Will always calls a mood for stirring up drama. Was in it already, I suppose, what with him in hospital and being psyched up for playing Gertrude in Brighton. Mountain out of molehill time. That's all it was, really.*

It sounds so innocent. Why hasn't she told this innocent story to Will? Her reluctance to tell him seems suddenly quite deranged. She cannot imagine how she had been thinking and feeling. It is as if she has lost touch with herself, certainly with the self she had been only a few hours ago.

She says, 'I must have been mad,' and when Gemma looks at her in the mirror, surprised and enquiring, lies swiftly, 'I mean, I have forgotten my cheque book. I changed my handbag and didn't look . . . I do hope I have enough cash.'

*   *   *

Will and Alice are doing the seating plan for the birthday party when Coral comes home. She has brought lunch with her from Marks and Spencer. She says, as she comes into the kitchen, 'I got those delicious crab cakes, and salad, and there's still some of that nice cheese from last night. Haven't you finished that table plan, Will?'

'Harder than you think,' Will says. 'Not just who's next to who, but who's facing who across that big table. Who's deaf and who isn't. Well, some of the people none of us know. His banker from Zurich. And a pair of distant cousins he was determined to include for some reason. The wife is the daughter of Martin Mudd, a well-known psychiatrist, so Alice tells me. Dead now, of course. Though why I say *of course*, I don't know. He'd only be about Father's age, wouldn't he, Alice?'

He smiles at his sister, at his wife. Coral is looking much better, not just the fresh hair-do, but more relaxed, happier. She smiles back at him in an open and friendly manner that makes him realise how strained, haggard, almost old, she has been looking lately.

He wants to tell her about the roses at once but is inhibited. What has been joyful news to him may seem insulting to her. She will divine from his haste that he had suspected her of keeping *something* secret from him, even if it is not necessarily a lover. No, he must drop it into the conversation later on, during lunch perhaps, casually . . .

Alice says, 'Your hair looks lovely, Coral darling. But then it always does. Every time I see you, I think you have grown more beautiful. Don't you think so, Will? Wearing well, isn't she?'

'Remarkably so,' Will says gravely, catching Coral's eye. 'Lasting quality, I recognised it the moment I saw her. Like Father, I have an eye for a good investment.'

Alice looks uncomprehending. 'What *do* you mean, darling? Oh, never mind. I was telling you about Martin Mudd. He wrote a seminal book on the types of psychoses that are sometimes produced by LSD and cannabis resin. It's still regarded as the best work on the subject. He and Father must have been fairly close at one time. I know Father consulted him about Mother. Though Martin would have been quite old by then, wouldn't he? Not necessarily retired, I suppose. Doctors went on working much longer then, now all they want to do is get out of the NHS before the strain kills them. Understandably.'

'Yes.' Will is watching Coral. He can bear it no longer. 'Oh. Before I forget. Father rang up. He wanted to know if Molly had got the flowers he sent. The roses, congratulating her on her performance on television. He said he'd forgotten to put a card with them. I said you thought they were lovely.'

Coral starts to laugh. She clutches her hands to her ribs as if laughing is painful, and then, to his amazement, he sees she is crying. She holds out her hands to him, weeping, and he puts his arms round her and holds her.

CHAPTER FIFTEEN

Silas had often missed Aunt, but never so poignantly. He had no wish to imagine her comments on Effie's behaviour. It was help with the girls that he wanted. He suspected they knew more than they were likely to tell him and certainly more than he wanted to hear from them, but even if they were prepared for Effie leaving him for another man, the realisation that this meant she was leaving them too might come as more of a shock. He

211

thought grimly of what he saw now as Effie's false protestations of love for her 'babies' at the outbreak of war. She had always been given to extravagant displays of affection, hugging and kissing and presents: Hannah and Alice must have grown up confident that she loved them.

Aunt would have known what to do for them now, how to comfort them: adolescent females were not the mystery to her that they were to him. She loved both the girls but she had always been especially protective of Hannah, whom she seemed to think needed particular attention. 'She's all passion and feeling, Silas, more than she can manage to handle. More dependent on other people's opinion of her than Alice, which makes her life harder. Sometimes, you know, she reminds me of Molly.'

This comparison was unreal to Silas. A womanly delusion, he thought. Aunt, in her dotage, was indulging, uncharacteristically, in the specifically feminine occupation of searching for signs of kinship in brothers, sisters, nieces, nephews, cousins, the family nose, a smile, a fleeting look, leading her in this instance into absurdity. How could there be any connection between his graceful, talented sister and his awkward, irrational daughter?

But it set him thinking. At Hannah's age, Molly had been grown-up, no longer a child, about to set off to RADA and cheap lodgings in the city. Perhaps Hannah was in fact older than she seemed to him; old enough, anyway, to take charge of her sister in London while he discovered what was happening at home in Norwich. In her letter Effie had said she was leaving 'as soon as Dolly comes home from France'. Tomorrow? Next week? Typical of Effie to be vague about practical matters. She had not mentioned her daughters, not even to send them her love. Perhaps that was to her credit: she was ashamed of her hypocrisy. But he doubted it. She had simply not thought of them: they were with their father in London, out of sight, out of mind. She cared nothing for them as she cared nothing for him. Beside her fancy over-sexed American with a silly girl's name, her family was nothing to her.

He thought, I could kill her.

He told Hannah and Alice that their mother was 'feeling a bit under the weather' and had suggested she and Alice stayed in London for a few more days, a week, perhaps. Now the European war was over it was a good opportunity to explore their capital city. Bombed and battered and broken, it was still beautiful, and now the blackout was over the lights would be on again.

They listened in silence. Alice looked at him, still-faced and serious, an expression that gave nothing away. Hannah coloured up, her cheeks burning, and once or twice seemed to

213

have trouble stifling unsuitable laughter. But her eyes were liquid with pain.

She burst out, words tumbling, 'Don't worry, Father, we'll be all right, you don't have to worry about anything, I'll keep house and Alice will help me, it'll be fun, won't it, Alice? We're quite used to it, helping Mother. We didn't bring enough clothes for much more than a few days, but we can manage. I mean, I can wash some things out and dry them in the boiler cupboard. And Mother put our ration books in our suitcases. So I can go shopping for you if you give me some money.'

'Whatever you think you need,' Silas said. It surprised him that neither girl had asked what was wrong with her mother. Then he realised, with a shock that turned him dizzy, that they almost certainly did understand what had happened or, at least, understood enough not to ask further questions. It made him uneasy with them, especially with Hannah who watched him all the time, intently and sadly. There were only two small, dark bedrooms in the basement and so when they were all three in the house, they were usually together in the kitchen, which was also their living room; whenever Silas turned round, or looked up from a book or a newspaper, Hannah's mournful eyes were upon him.

He wondered if either of them had spoken to Effie. But he didn't ask. He had no answer when he telephoned from the Ministry.

Although he knew it was foolish, he thought he could tell from the desolate sound of the ring that the house was deserted. She had gone, as she had said she would. 'Dolly' had come back from France, perhaps the day she had posted the letter, and he would never see her again. Nor would Hannah or Alice. She would remember her children's birthdays for a while perhaps, but that would be all . . .

It was five days before he went to Norwich. Five days of silence. 'Never put off till tomorrow what you should do today,' was what Aunt always said. Well, he had put it off for five days, trapped by a mix of cowardice, superstition and hope. He couldn't bear to be physically faced with her absence; as long as he didn't actually see the empty house he could imagine she might still be in it.

He was glad that the train was slow. He walked from the station like an old man. He stood at the gate and gazed at the small, neglected front garden. Then he gathered his courage. There was no light showing. He put his key in the door and it creaked as it opened. He stood in the hall, which smelt stale and dusty. He closed the front door behind him and switched the light on. Apart from that *click*, there was no sound in the house.

He pushed open the door into the sitting room. Empty, as was the dining room and the kitchen. There were the remains of a meal on the kitchen table, several meals, in fact. A

215

bottle of milk, half full, its cap missing, a bowl with a last spoonful of porridge crusted in it, a couple of plates with the remains of what might have been dried egg and tomato, half a dozen slices of bread, stiff with age.

This was unlike Effie. She was hardly an enthusiastic housekeeper but she was finicky about food and hygiene. He had never known her to leave dirty cups and plates on a table. Perhaps she had reckoned that since she was leaving him, she might as well leave her mess for him to clear up!

Anger seized him. This sluttish behaviour showed her contempt for him. No doubt the bathroom would be filthy too; towels chucked on the floor, used sanitary napkins, toothpaste spat out to dry hard in the basin . . .

His rage inflated, hammering in his chest as he raced up the stairs. He flung open the door to the bathroom to find towels neat on their rails, toothbrushes in holders, washbasin sparkling clean. Oh, so she had cleaned up before she left, had she? Did she think a bit of housewifely care would soften him towards her? Why should she care anyway? His *sad, bad, but still loving wife.* Was that how she'd signed herself? Why hadn't he kept the letter? He could have stuffed it in her mouth, made her eat her words. Only she wasn't here to be punished. She'd walked out on him, left him for an American soldier called Dolly.

He looked at his face in the glass over the

basin and saw it, red and contorted, his still thick and dark hair streaked over his forehead. He said, 'Why shouldn't she leave you, you coarse, ugly bugger?'

He thought how delighted Gladys Ogilvie would be, were she still alive, and snorted with laughter. He turned to the lavatory, unbuttoned his flies and, for the first time in his life, emptied his bladder without first closing the bathroom door.

Behind him, Effie said, 'Silas.'

She was standing in the doorway, swaying a little. She was wearing a white nightdress, her hair was tangled and loose and her eyes were swollen and muzzy with sleep.

He said, ashamed, 'I'm sorry. I thought— that is, I didn't know you were here or I wouldn't have . . . I mean, I would have shut the door. I thought the house was empty.' He shook the last drops from his penis and turned away to fasten his trousers.

She made a sound somewhere between a sob and a giggle. She said, 'Oh, Silas, how like you to fuss. At a time like this.'

She was actually smiling. Not much of a smile, but a smile. It fed his anger; he felt it swelling hotly inside him. If she didn't stop smiling, he thought he might hit her. He said, 'I thought you'd be gone.'

He turned back to her and saw she was not smiling now. She looked pale and ill. She said, drearily, 'As you can see, I'm still here. I'm

217

sorry I upset you for nothing.'

'Upset?' he repeated. '*Upset*! Is that what you call it? You break a man's life into pieces and you call it *upset*?'

It was plain what had happened. The man had left her. The war was over, he'd had his fun and would be going home to the American girlfriend he had been writing love letters to all along. Or going home to his wife . . .

He said, 'Dumped you, has he? I expect there's going to be a lot of that sort of thing. Soldiers going home to their wives and children and dumping their girlfriends. Their temporary, wartime girlfriends. Their conveniences. That's all you were to your Dolly. A sexual convenience.'

She said, 'He's dead.'

He didn't take it in immediately. 'I suppose you think you can come crawling back, do you? And Muggins here is supposed to be grateful?'

'Oh, Silas,' she said. 'Silas . . .'

She was weeping now. She turned away and trailed across the landing. When he followed her, she was collapsed by the side of the bed, arms flung across it, head on her arms. She was groaning rather than crying, as if she had cramp in her stomach. Or keening, he thought. Keening over her dead.

He said, bewildered, 'But the war's over.'

Unless the man had been sent to the Far East. But Effie had said he was in France. Her letter had said, 'when Dolly comes back from

France'. That was the sense, if not the exact wording.

She threw back her head and wailed. Screamed at him. 'A mine, you half-witted ape. He stepped on a mine . . .'

She doubled up, arms wrapped round her body, rocking backwards and forwards. He scooped her up in his arms to put her on the bed and memory flicked him, light as a hair on his throat. She was easier to lift than his mother had been, but of course, he was stronger and older.

He touched her tentatively in the soft bend of her arm where she always liked to be stroked, and she didn't reject him. He thought again of his mother, consciously this time. At least his wife was alive. He said, 'How did it happen? Do you want to tell me?'

She told him, not all at once, but over the next hour or so while he sat beside her. Dolly—Silas never asked her his real name—and what she called his 'lot' had been clearing up a German command post that had been booby-trapped when they retreated, mines hidden on or beneath the bodies of soldiers. Dolly had bent over this German officer to cover his dead, shattered face with a handkerchief and the mine had exploded. One of Dolly's friends, Effie didn't know the man's name, had come to see her when he got back to England four days ago. She had been expecting Dolly, her suitcase packed and ready in the hall.

She rolled over on the bed and said, into Silas's lap, 'You know, I thought at first he'd come to take me to Dolly, wasn't that stupid? I should have known, really I should, because he looked so tired, quite dirty, too, as if he hadn't had time to wash or change his clothes, and of course he would have done that, wouldn't he, out of respect, if he'd come to fetch me instead of Dolly, just because Dolly was busy?'

* * *

She was silly, as always; the innocent centre of her own universe. It made Silas less vengeful if not entirely magnanimous. He stoked the kitchen boiler and when there was enough hot water, ran a bath and persuaded her to get into it. When she said she was feeling too weak, she couldn't be bothered, she just wanted to sleep, he told her she smelt, which was true. While she was bathing, he went downstairs and washed the dishes. He found stale bread, a bag of sprouting potatoes and a tin of pilchards in the larder. He boiled the potatoes and mashed them with the remains of the milk that would be sour by tomorrow, added pepper and salt and put them to keep warm in the oven. He opened the tin of fish and cut slices from the loaf to make toast under the grill. There was no wine, or beer, but he found a bottle of sweet sherry in the sideboard in the dining room and put it on the kitchen table with two glasses beside it. He laid the table with plates and cutlery and picked a single rose from the garden to put in the silver holder that Aunt had left him. When she came downstairs in her cotton wrapper these preparations made her cry.

'Oh,' she said, weeping, 'oh, Siley, I've been so horrible to you and you're so good to me, I don't deserve it.'

'No.'

What else did she expect him to say? That he was her devoted slave? That he sorrowed with her for the death of her lover, and would do his best for the rest of his life to help her to bear it? Something like that, he supposed, and was coldly amused by the way her eyes reproached him over her glass of sherry.

He said, 'We have to decide what to do. We have to think of the girls first of all. I intend to make an offer for the lease of the London house but it will be some time before we can start building work and in the meantime the basement isn't really a suitable home for them, far too poky and dark. So they will have to come back here, I'm afraid. If that is inconvenient for you, I'm sorry.'

She said incredulously, 'Do you mean you think I don't want my own daughters here, in this house? Or are you turning me out?'

'Forgive me. I had assumed you might still want to go.'

Pleased with this exchange, Silas turned to the stove and lit the grill. And waited.

He heard the *thump* as she put her glass down on the table. She came up behind him and touched him on the shoulder. She said, coaxingly, 'Oh, Siley darling, how *can* you? You know what I've been going through. Oh, perhaps you don't. What I felt for Dolly was like nothing I'd ever felt before, like a great wild wind sweeping through me. A force of nature, something primeval. Since I heard he was dead, I've been torn apart . . .'

He shook her hand off his shoulder and she went back to her seat at the table and threw her head back and howled, 'Oh, I do miss him so much, in my *bowels* I miss him . . .'

He said, disgusted, 'You and your novels! Which one taught you that pretty language? Do you want your pilchards on toast, or on their own with the mashed potatoes?'

'You don't expect me to eat anything after that, do you?'

He was interested to see that she was simply angry now. Her eyes were dry and blazing.

He heaped his own plate and sat down at the table. He smiled at her. 'I hope you don't mind if I start. I'm rather hungry. Would you like another glass of sherry? You seem to have finished that one rather quickly.'

She thrust her glass towards him and he filled it until it brimmed over. He said, 'I hope you are not becoming an alcoholic.'

She threw the sherry in his face. He laughed at her, the sticky stuff dripping down his nose and cheeks. He said, 'I asked for that, didn't I? But you did goad me. I may not have your capacity for passion but perhaps it was inadvisable to point it out to me.'

He ate the pilchards and potato, keeping his eyes on his plate. When he had finished he said, 'Perhaps you would clear up, it's your turn, I think. I am going to my bed. You are welcome to join me, but I shall understand if you prefer to sleep in Hannah's room. Or Alice's, of course. We will discuss our daughters and their future in the morning.'

Suddenly, he was wearier than he had ever been in his life. He went to sleep at once and slept the night through. When he woke, at six in the morning, the birds were singing outside in the garden and Effie was lying beside him. She was lying on her side, on the coverlet not under the bedclothes. She was awake, watching him, and when she put out her hand to him, it felt icy cold.

She had been crying, her face was blubbered with tears, and when she saw that his eyes were open she began to sob tiredly, like an exhausted child. He put his arm round her and she wept into his shoulder. She said, 'Don't be angry with me, you once said you'd look after me for ever, you promised me and I believed you, please keep your promise, I'll do my best, I really will, and I do love you, it was different with Dolly, not better, I've been awake all night, thinking and worrying, I'm so dreadfully tired and unhappy, please look after me, please . . .'

On and on until he could no longer bear it. He got out of the bed and rolled her into the warm place where he had been sleeping and drew covers over her. He said, 'It's all right, everything's all right, go to sleep now. I'll ring the office and the girls and stay with you today. I'll look after you, today and all the days that come after.'

CHAPTER SIXTEEN

He believed (as he still believes) that he did his best. He did it out of duty, he had 'put his hand to the plough', as Aunt would have said. And, though he would never again tell Effie he loved her, he did it out of love as well. He was angry and bitterly hurt, but once the anger had diminished, he began to excuse her. She was a wild, natural creature, trapped inside a personality that did not include the usual freedoms of moral choice. She had been encouraged from birth to believe that what she wanted she should have, that her desires were all-important, not subject to the constraints of ordinary accepted behaviour.

This is what Silas told himself because it

224

allowed him to go on loving her as he wanted to. She had not changed, she was still the beautiful child he had fallen in love with. He also told himself that it was her determination to follow the impulses of her heart that had allowed her to deceive her parents, to give herself to him in the churchyard. Or put it another way (as he sometimes did when resentment took hold of him), she might be a greedy, self-absorbed slut, but if she had been a good girl, a chaste young lady, a loving and dutiful daughter, she would never have married him.

And the apparent success of their marriage was important to Silas. Always had been, still was. It was not just that he was a man who preferred to rewrite the past rather than to regret it. Effie was a fine feather in his cap, a well-bred, good-looking woman he was proud to parade in front of his business acquaintances, an ornament who would grace the Belgravia house when the work on it was finished.

Even if Effie had objected to the move, she was in no position to argue and in fact accepted the prospect of change with some grace, showing intelligent interest in the architect's drawings and commendable patience over the lengthy and tedious business of submitting planning applications. For Silas, the fact that they would be unable to move for at least a year, which meant he could continue to live alone in the basement and only go to

Norwich at weekends was an unexpected relief: he found, to his surprise and dismay, that he was physically shrinking from Effie, unwilling to touch her, even to brush against her if they passed on the stairs. When he was home they still shared the same bed, for the girls' sake, he told himself, so they could understand that whatever had happened between their parents, things were now back to normal, but also because he was ashamed to admit, even to himself, how he felt. It seemed weak and unmanly. In bed with Effie, he lay rigidly on the edge of the mattress. If she put out a hand to him, he feigned sleep.

Strangely—at least it seemed strange to him—when he realised she was pregnant, his distaste for her body left him entirely. That was a Sunday morning in late October. He was lying in bed, not yet quite awake, stretching his legs and arms, sleepily grateful to find the bed empty. She came naked into the room, from the bathroom presumably, and went to the window to draw back the curtains. Only an autumnal greyness filtered in, but it was enough to display the curve of her body.

Although he was unaware of it, he must have made a sound because she turned sharply He couldn't see her face, but he saw that she crossed her hands protectively over her belly.

He said, 'Don't move. You make a charmingly fecund picture, standing there against the light.'

226

He was amazed to hear his own voice sounding so calm, so dispassionate. He said, 'Am I allowed to know when it's due?'

'Have you only just noticed? I'm nearly five months.' She stopped, briefly, then said, angrily, 'Why else do you suppose I was going off with him?'

He didn't answer for a minute. Her defiance was predictable. She must have rehearsed this moment: she had not been taken by surprise.

At last he said, 'You may have noticed that I have been avoiding close contact with you. That obviously included not looking at you too intently. If I thought anything, I may have thought you'd been putting on weight and wouldn't be pleased if I mentioned it. As for *going off with him*, as you put it, do forgive me, but I understood you were in the grip of an uncontrollable passion of a kind a simple-minded, crude fellow like me would be unable to comprehend.'

She whispered, 'Don't be cruel, Silas.'

'Do the girls know?' He hoped he sounded indifferent.

'I suppose they may have noticed. I haven't said anything to them, if that's what you mean.'

'Do you intend to?'

She began to dress, putting on her clothes without making any attempt to conceal her new awkwardness from him, and he was suddenly, unexpectedly, aroused by her soft, rounded body.

When she was in her petticoat, standing in front of her dressing-table, she said, 'It depends on you, doesn't it?'

'What do you mean?'

'Oh, God! That's obvious, isn't it?'

'Not to me.'

A theatrically impatient sigh. 'Do you want them to know the name of its father?'

She was more anxious than she sounded, he thought. He said, 'I can't discuss this while you're on the other side of the room, primping in front of the mirror. Come here if you want to talk about it. Don't worry, I won't hit you. I dare say it ought to be the proper masculine approach in these circumstances, but I'm not sure that I have the energy or the inclination.'

She crossed the room slowly. He was almost unbearably excited. He said, 'There's no chance it could be mine, is there? Oh, don't bother to answer. You never wanted to, not for months. I thought you'd gone off me. Well, you had, of course, it just never occurred to me that another man might have been rumbling over the points. But if the idea appeals to you, there's no reason why Hannah and Alice shouldn't be allowed to assume I've been playing box and cox with your lover.'

She sat on the edge of the bed, her eyes fixed on him. He saw she was frightened and a wave of love and pity swept over him.

He held out his hand to her. He said, 'Be a

good girl, there's nothing to be afraid of. Just take your clothes off again, and get into bed with me.'

*   *   *

He had expected to be disgusted with himself afterwards and was surprised to find he felt perfectly comfortable. He had been careful because of the pregnancy but he thought Effie had not been unwilling, even if she had been more passive than usual. He didn't mind that: it made him feel stronger, more in control and, to his initial surprise, in the next weeks he found sex with Effie an easier, more relaxed and straightforward activity than he had known it before. If he recognised that this was because he was no longer nervous of offending or hurting her, he put the slightly shaming knowledge away and told himself that up to now he had been a too considerate and worshipful husband and knowing she had taken a lover had liberated him. Nowadays he could put his own pleasure first.

Neither of them mentioned this to the other. All they talked about together was the reconstruction of the London house, Hannah's Higher School Certificate results and her Oxford entrance examination, whether Alice would do well at St Paul's School for Girls once they were living in London, and if they could possibly make the move while the building work was still going on. He was pleased that Effie seemed healthy and content. He made sure she kept her doctor's appointments and was booked into a maternity hospital. No more home births after Hannah.

Having done his family duty, he was relieved to be otherwise busily occupied. He was winding up his work at the Ministry, a job that he had never seen as anything other than clerical, making sure that the right tools, in this case machine tools, raw materials, ammunition, engine and weapon parts, arrived at the right time in the right hands, and was surprised to discover that what he had done was thought to have been sufficiently useful for him to be offered a knighthood in the New Year's Honours list. Although he knew Aunt would have been pleased, in spite of her dislike for the aristocracy which, to a milder extent, included the monarchy, Aunt was dead, and the thought of how it would have pleased Gladys Ogilvie and, indeed, how it would please Effie to be Lady Mudd, was decisive. He turned it down and told no one.

He might have told Hans but there had been no word from him since the European war ended. Until now, they had been in touch whenever Hans could manage, usually by letter but occasionally in person, when he could get 'a lift' as he called it; fishing-boats, small naval craft. Hans Jensen was one link in a chain that sent back to England some of the airmen shot down over Europe, which was why the Navy was willing to give him safe passage, but his main operation was the rescue of Danish Jews. For some of them, he could arrange visas; others made their way to Silas's basement until he could find jobs for them; doctors working as porters in hospitals, bankers and lawyers as sweepers in factories. The old people, the ones who had refused to leave Denmark, unable to believe the German occupation would harm them, were harder to help. Hans Jensen's wife was German and Hans was working in the Danish Embassy; since the occupying forces were intent on being conciliatory, it was not difficult for the Jensens to meet and mix with German officers, members of the Gestapo.

The elderly Danish Jews had all been sent to Teresienstadt. 'They could have got out to Sweden earlier on if they had been sensible,' Hans had told Silas. 'Now there is nothing to be done, except—how do you say it in English?— suck up to the buggers? The Germans. Persuade them to let us send medicines and food and some smaller comforts. It means, I am afraid, that my poor wife and I have to spend far too much time being agreeable to our enemies. I have to tell you, some of our fellow countrymen sometimes look at me strangely.'

Hans had laughed then, quite unperturbed, as if how other people might look at his unpatriotic social activities was a bit of a joke. When he stopped hearing from him Silas had wondered, though not very often or very seriously. Europe was at peace now; there was plenty of time. He wrote to the safe address Hans had given him but no answer came back. He didn't write again. Once Effie's child was born and she and the children were settled in London, he would go to Copenhagen to find his friend Hans, meet his brave wife, his children. There was no urgent need. It was simply a pleasure to look forward to. Silas thought of Hans, straightforwardly and very simply, as a best friend; like the friends he had made in his school years, the gamekeeper's son he had shared boyhood adventures with and lost in the last war, the Great War. The adventures he had shared with Hans were more serious but there had been an element of quixotic boyish excitement in them; he had to remind himself sometimes that Hans was in danger and he was not.

Now that the war was safely over, he would have liked to tell Effie about Hans, prepare her for meeting him, but an uneasy feeling that she might think he was trying to present himself to her in a more dashing light than a cuckolded husband prevented him. Besides, she was engrossed in her pregnancy, particularly since the doctor had told her she must remember that at her age childbirth was likely to be difficult if not positively hazardous. On his instruction she lay down every afternoon after lunch until it was time to bath and dress for dinner, a habit which was to continue for the rest of her life and one, Silas privately thought, that contributed to her horrific and lengthy labour.

Too weak to help herself, the midwife told him when the long night was over. 'Too old, really, your poor wife,' she said, 'though Doctor says he's seen more elderly mothers lately. It's the war, he says. She'll be all right, though, a few hours yet but no need to worry. I must say you're one of the few fathers I've known to actually sit it out. Would you like a nice cup of tea?'

'I'd like to see my wife,' Silas said.

She looked at him, he thought unfavourably. She said, 'I don't think that's a good idea, do you? I suppose I could ask Doctor.'

'Yes, please do that,' Silas said.

This time her expression was unequivocally hostile. But she went into the labour ward and reappeared almost immediately, beckoning. 'Five minutes,' she said. 'Just to reassure yourself, we don't want to put her off the job, do we?'

There were electric fans near the bed, but Effie was tossing and wailing. 'I'm so hot, Silas. Hold my hand. Do I look awful?'

He held her hot hand and told her she looked beautiful as she always did, though in fact she looked lined and crumpled, like a piece of damp tissue paper. A pain tore at her and she writhed with it, digging her nails into his palm, and letting out a long moaning cry 'I'm sorry, but I can't bear it, Silas, it's like being torn in two.'

The midwife was bending over her, dabbing her forehead. 'Now, dearie, don't upset your poor hubby, he's upset enough as it is.' And to Silas, 'It's not as bad as it looks, I told you it wasn't a good idea, didn't I?'

'I am going to stay here as long as she wants me to,' Silas said.

And he was appalled. He had not been present except at the very early stage in the birth of his daughters; what he remembered most clearly was Effie sitting up when it was all over, pale but pretty, in a fluffy bedjacket. Had it been like this for her before? It struck him, with a sudden, cruel shaft of humour, that she was paying a fair price for her infidelity. He found her agonised groaning hard to bear all the same and was infinitely relieved when the consultant came, took one look at Effie, and ordered him out.

He waited on a shiny leather sofa. Someone—another nurse—brought him a cup of tea. She said, 'I've put sugar in, you look as if you need it.' But they called him before he had time to drink it.

Effie watched him hazily from the bed. 'Chloroform,' the doctor said. 'She'll be lively enough in a minute. I thought I might introduce you to your son.'

He was young, this doctor, pink-faced and cheery. Silas smiled, to please him, and took the baby in his arms. He wondered why he felt so little. He told himself, Another man's child, and expected a rush of rage and resentment. But it didn't come. He said, to Effie, 'He's a lovely boy. Bigger than the girls, quite a weight to carry. Shall I put him beside you?'

She rolled her head from side to side fretfully. She said, 'I don't want to look at him, I don't *want* him. Take him away, don't let him near me.'

*　　*　　*

They said it was natural, she'd had a bad time, give her a day or so. But her revulsion, if that's what it was, it seemed more like petulance to Silas, persisted long after the two weeks in hospital, even after she was at home in the London mansion flat they had rented while the house in Belgravia was being prepared for them. He had hired a nurse for the month, a middle-aged woman who seemed motherly and sensible, not the sort of stupid sloven to drug a child with a flannel that had been on the gas stove. He explained that the baby was being bottle-fed because his mother had been exhausted by the birth, and that was probably why she was showing so little interest in him. The nurse murmured, 'Very likely,' and took the cot into her own room.

When she was out, in the evenings, he tried to persuade Effie at least to look at the child, hold him for a few minutes. He had no success. She would take him briefly in her arms and then hand him back, shaking her head in what Silas began to comprehend was genuine distress. Towards the end of the month, the nurse asked for a night off for a family wedding. Hannah and Alice were home, and Silas said they could manage. He moved the cot into the bedroom and put it on his side of the bed. And the boy woke in the night.

He screamed and screamed. Silas picked him up and walked round the room with him. He was briefly quiet, and then began wailing again, desperate, small, hiccuping sobs. 'I'll get a bottle,' Silas said, and put him on the bed, beside Effie. When he came back, Will was back in his cot, face screwed up and scarlet, fat legs kicking in fury.

Silas picked him up and began to feed him. 'For God's sake,' he said, 'couldn't you have held him for a minute?' And then, bitterly, 'You loved his father, didn't you? More than you loved me was the implication. Why can't you love your fancy man's son?'

'I don't know,' was all Effie said. 'I don't know.'

It was all she could say, perhaps, but he couldn't stay in the room with her afterwards. He went down to the living room and sat on the sofa for the rest of the night, cradling the sleeping boy, whispering to him, 'It's all right, old chap, I'm here, and Hannah, and Alice, and your mother will come round in the end, I think I can promise you.'

CHAPTER SEVENTEEN

Nine o'clock in the evening preceding his birthday, Silas is speaking to Coral. 'You're quite sure the boy is well enough for this do tomorrow? No need to come if he's not fit. Not to say I wouldn't be disappointed, you understand, but his health is more important than an old man's vanity.'

Coral, her hand over the mouthpiece, whispers to Will and Alice, sitting late over dinner: 'He wants to know if "the boy" is up to the strain of the Birthday. Does the boy want to duck out of it?'

Will shakes his head, smiling. Coral says, 'No, he's fine, Daddy. He wouldn't miss it for anything.'

'That's all right, then. I worry about him. Always been a bit of a weakling. Catches everything going.'

'Not everything, Daddy! He hasn't had polio, hepatitis, blackwater fever . . .'

'Whassay? Not picking you up.'

Coral winks at Will, who shakes his head again, warning her not to be frivolous. She

237

says, loudly, 'I was just saying that although he may have several things wrong with him, he's basically healthy. Chip off the old block, Daddy.'

'Ah.'

'Good genes go a long way,' Coral says pleasantly.

Silence for perhaps twenty seconds, then Silas says, 'I know there's a lot of talk about that sort of thing nowadays. It's the sort of thing Alice deals in. Have a good night, Coral, my dear. See you tomorrow.'

*   *   *

He had said to Effie, 'Just one thing, and no more. The last time we mention it. The boy must never know.'

She had answered him with a barely perceptible nod but he was satisfied. Since they had moved to London she had no close women friends. Who would she tell? The girls? Will himself?

That was the only real danger that Silas could see. She might be tempted to tell the boy when he reached adolescence, to punish him for whatever harm she thought he had done her. Even as Will grew older and handsomer, a good-mannered, delightful boy, she remained distant with him. She allowed him to kiss her cheek but since that was the only affection she had ever shown him, Silas hoped the boy would assume it was the normal attitude of a modest mother to her growing son. And, of course, since Will was born, Effie had been reclusive and delicate; only naturally so, Silas was given to understand by their elderly family doctor, for a woman who had given birth so late in her life.

'Mother isn't very strong, you know, she needs a lot of rest,' he told Will, on the occasions he found him playing alone in his bedroom, *keeping quiet* as he had been told to do by Mrs Larkspur or Mrs Matthews or Mrs Hunt, whichever kindly lady was on duty at the moment. And 'I know,' Will would answer. 'That's why I'm keeping quiet, because Mother is sleeping.'

She slept. She bought clothes. What she bought the clothes for, Silas wondered. His fancy that she would do him credit as a hostess and companion had turned out to be foolish: she bought pretty clothes and hung them in the closets, or put them away in the handsome cedar chest she had fetched from Edinburgh when her mother died. Sometimes he would ask people to dinner and she would sit at the table looking beautiful, but although she laughed and talked, a lot of what she said was inconsequential and she would frequently disappear half-way through the meal and not come back again. When the guests had gone he would find her still fully dressed, fast asleep on the bed, drunk and snoring.

He had no one he felt able to speak to about her. He had no one to whom he was close enough any longer. Hans was dead, had killed himself at the end of the war when he was warned that he would be prosecuted as a collaborator. The injustice pained Silas almost more than the loss of his friend. It stained the world round him, blotting out decency, courage and honour. It didn't affect his working life, his business sense, he still knew how to hire and keep the best people, but he lost his nerve when it came to dealing with anyone on a more personal level. It made him shy and gruff with his children and when Effie refused to leave the house, refused to get out of bed, when she no longer seemed to remember him, he was helpless.

It was Hannah who finally insisted that something was done. 'I'm sorry, I think Mother should see a doctor. You've been wonderful with her, we all know that, but it's professional help she needs now.'

It seemed a shaming thing. He muttered, 'If you must. As long as you don't tell the boy. No need for him to know, is there?'

'All right, Father. Though I think—well, never mind. Julius says, what about Martin Mudd? Isn't he a sort of distant cousin or something? A good psychiatrist, Julius says.'

It was then Silas admitted Effie had gone where he could not follow her. And he knew he had finally failed her.

It tugs his heart still. He puts down the telephone after speaking to Coral and is stricken with sadness. They say all this stuff about genes nowadays. If he had only insisted she told him all she knew about Dolly's family, or if he had got in touch with the American friend who had brought the bad news to her, he might have been able to find out if there was anything he should watch out for in Will. He has no idea how he might have set about it, nor what he could have done if he had discovered there was a history of this or that illness; it is only part of the grief and guilt he feels when he thinks of his Effie. He feels guilty about the times he half hoped she would finish her life as she threatened to do, take the pills, hang herself, get out of his life before he went mad as well. And grief, of course, stabs him when he remembers her sad, puzzled eyes looking up at him. 'Who are you? Do I know you?' And heartbreakingly, 'Don't be cross with me, will you? I've been such a good girl today.'

'No point, no point,' he mutters, walking slowly across his comfortable room in his club, wondering if he should put out fresh pyjamas in honour of the birthday tomorrow and deciding against it. In a sudden moment of weariness, he longs for it all to be over, better still, for it not to happen. If death should come for him tonight he would welcome it for himself, and tomorrow's guests might not be so sorry: they could have a better time without him sitting there, the deaf old fool, the skull at the feast.

The picture that rises up in his mind makes him chuckle. Hannah would have particular difficulty in putting on the right facial expression: deep sorrow properly modified by the contemplation of her father's long, fulfilled life. He empties his pockets, his coins, his handkerchief, his magnifying glass, the pretty compass in a velvet case Bella gave him, takes off his watch, and then puts it on again. He won't have a shower tonight. Although he can't get into bed for a while because the maid has not yet brought his nightly Thermos of iced water, and he doesn't care to be seen by her in a state of undress, he can clean his teeth (which are all his own still) and empty his bowels and his bladder so that given a decent run of luck he won't have to get up in the night.

The bathroom is small but well lit and has an excellent bath with sensibly placed handles for getting in and out, which Silas has only used once; an occasion when he slipped suddenly, one minute standing at one end of the bath, under the shower, the next sitting in a couple of inches of soapy water. There had been no point in not taking advantage of such an unforeseen pleasure, so he had run a good hot bath and soaked himself agreeably for at least half an hour before he faced the grim prospect of struggling up and out of what was too much like a coffin for his liking. There was a bell, he had noticed on this occasion, a string to pull for just this sort of emergency, but he would have died rather than make use of it.

He chuckles again—he often chuckles at his thoughts when he is alone—as he lowers his trousers and sits on the lavatory, which is conveniently placed between the bath and the washbasin so there are surfaces on either side on which he can place his spectacles, his pen, the book he is reading, any small item that might otherwise fall out of his pockets.

'At what point would you rather *not* die?' he asks himself, and answers, aloud, 'When it's too late, you fool. Point of no return. When you've reached the stage of being too weak to shout, call someone, let alone pull a bell.'

For some reason, perhaps because he'd had more than usual to drink with his solitary and early dinner, bracing himself for the ordeal tomorrow, this makes him laugh immoderately. Laughing so hard gives him hiccups, quite a painful attack. With his left hand, he stretches out for the tooth-glass, which is half full of water but just out of his reach on the far side of the wash-basin— glasses of water not being in the catalogue of things he is normally likely to need when on

243

the lavatory. His left arm feels odd to him, not much strength in it. He leans a bit further, loses his balance and falls off the lavatory.

A stupid miscalculation. Better to have endured the hiccups, which are one of the minor discomforts that occasionally plague him. Too late now. He has ended up squeezed between the lavatory bowl and the pedestal of the wash-basin, a space he would have thought too narrow to accommodate him before he actually found himself in it. He begins to laugh again at this foolish thought, but stops when he tries to move his left leg. It doesn't seem to respond to the usual command.

No laughing matter.

Carefully, slowly, he tests his other limbs. The left arm doesn't feel quite so good either, but his right arm is functioning normally; he manages to get hold of the far side of the lavatory bowl and pull himself up to a more comfortable, though hardly luxurious, sitting position. 'Getting there, getting there,' he says encouragingly, 'that's the ticket.' His right leg is working all right as well. He tells it to flex the foot, and it obeys him.

Bella would have had a good laugh at his plight. He'd had one or two funny turns while they were together; once, in the Grande Bretagne in Athens, he'd spent the night on the floor because she couldn't haul him up on to the bed and he wouldn't let her call the desk and ask for someone to help them. And he had been right not to give in. Bella had made him a luxurious nest on the floor with all the pillows and a soft fluffy blanket and he'd had a decent night and woken with all his parts in working order, even a fairly perky erection.

That had surprised the dear girl, he remembers now, but the memory doesn't produce even the ghost of a chuckle. His present situation is too humiliating. Only a sadist could be amused by it.

He has managed to shuffle forward, working with his right arm and his right buttock and heel, until he is out of his prison and resting in the comparative freedom of the bathroom floor. Now he can sit up, if in a lop-sided way, taking his weight on his right hand. The trouble is, if he lifts that hand from the floor to grab hold of the side of the bath, he will topple over. The bath is just that small distance too far away. His left arm is useless and his right is already trembling under his weight.

He could do with Bella now. She would fetch his stick. She would keep his spirits up. She'd be strong enough to support him while he made a grab for the side of the bath. She could help him get his trousers on. Then he would let her ring the emergency bell, not before. He would rather die than be found with his pants round his knees. Or would he? He recognises that this is the not the first time he has had this conversation with himself this evening and on this second occasion he finds it lacking in humour.

Someone is knocking on the bedroom door. Then a voice, a light voice, a pretty accent: it is the French girl tonight. 'Is it all right to come in? It's your water, sir.'

A pause. Then the creak of the old boards under the carpet as she crosses the room. He holds his breath. She will know he is in the bathroom, she will see the light under the door. She won't come in; even if she should try to, suspecting from his silence that something is wrong, he has locked the door as he always does. He realises too late that the locked door means he could safely call out to her, ask her to fetch a man, the night porter. The girl has, in fact, spoken, presumably in case he is listening, 'Good night, sir.' And the bedroom door closes.

Sir, he thinks. *Sir.* Perhaps he was a fool to turn down that knighthood. Bella would have loved it. He can hear her laughing now. Lady Mudd. Lady Muck. He had deprived her of an innocent pleasure just to be spiteful to the Ogilvies, mother and daughter . . .

He is puzzled suddenly. At the time Beaverbrook put him up for it, had he even *known* Bella? He decides he will work that out later; sometimes, if he forgets a thing, a date or a name, it will only sneak back into his mind if he doesn't try to remember. Turn to something else is the answer. For a moment he thinks, Molly will be pleased when I tell her I'm going to the Palace. Then, I've got something wrong here.

Molly is dead. That's what's wrong. Or is she? He hears her saying, calm and clear, 'It's all right, love, Molly's here. Grab hold of the side of that bath while you've still got the strength, you won't fall if you're quick. Anyway, it's the only thing to do, isn't it?'

He does as she tells him. He takes a bit of a tumble, thumping his shoulder painfully against the hard side of the bath, but he can hang on to the side now, with his right hand. More convenient, he thinks, if it were his left leg still working, better balance to have a functioning limb on each side, but accidents don't consider a person's convenience. He'll have to make do.

His sticks are resting against the door. Silly place to leave them, out of reach like that, next time he'll prop them between the wash-basin and the lavatory. At least he will be able to use a stick to unlock the door. Once he gets there.

Shuffle. Stop. Breathe. Shuffle. Right leg, right hand. Buttock sore. Never mind, rub it with Tiger Balm, that'll cure it. Davey now, Bella's boy, would laugh at that, he's a modern young doctor. Still, he doesn't know everything even if he has been to Cambridge . . .

Perhaps Aunt was right. Perhaps he should have gone to Cambridge as she wanted him to.

Then he might not have met Effie.

And his life would have been empty.

He has reached the door. He rests for a minute. He leans against the bath and reaches up. His arm is longer than he had reckoned, he slides the bolt easily. Opening the door is more difficult. His body is not exactly manoeuvrable. He addresses it, grumbling, aloud, 'All these years I've looked after you, fed you and watered you, let you rest when you wanted, what the hell are you doing letting me down now?'

Insulting his body cheers him considerably. He has got the door open and is shuffling off cold, hard tiles on to soft carpet. The bed is within crawling distance, and it is a low bed, a base and a mattress on castors. Winning post in sight. He manages to turn and move backwards, kicking his right leg out of his trousers. It'll be harder to get the left leg off but he'll have a go in a minute.

He is sweating a lot. He thinks, Home if not dry, which is one of Bella's coarser remarks that he thinks goes too far. Offends his sense of propriety. Not the sort of thing a woman should say. Or a man either, in his view, but Aunt had brought him up to be mealy-mouthed. Puritanical. Too late to change now.

The last stage is exhausting but one small triumph pleases him: his left trouser leg comes off as he gets his right leg well on the bed and manages to drag the inert left side of his body over the edge of the mattress. He lies on his face for a while, panting, then slowly rolls over and lies on his back. His tie seems to be tighter than usual, choking him, but he hasn't the energy to remove it. He closes his eyes and is asleep in a minute.

*   *   *

Something wakes him. He is lying on his bed. His mouth is dry, a desiccated dark cave. All the lights are on. Bewildered, he puts his hand to the knot of his tie. It must be late afternoon, he must have dropped off after lunch. That is why he is wearing his clothes. Though why are the lights on? It is light enough in the early afternoons even at this time of the year. And he is without his trousers. That's odd.

The telephone is ringing. It has been ringing some time. He grabs at it with his right hand and knocks several things off the night table.

Will says, 'Father? I haven't woken you, have I? It's only just after eleven. I know you like to watch the late news. I just wanted to reassure you that I'm absolutely fine, much looking forward to tomorrow, speech written and everything. Coral thought you were worrying in case I wasn't up to it. Father. Father?'

'I'm here,' Silas said. 'Just wasn't expecting . . . Made a bit of a doo-da grabbing the telephone.'

He had picked up the receiver with his right

249

hand. He had touched the knot of his tie with his left. He picks up his left hand and holds it up in front of him, wriggling his fingers.

Will says, 'You're all right, Father? Sorry if I . . .'

'No,' Silas says. 'Good to hear from you, Will. I'm just fine. See you tomorrow.'

CHAPTER EIGHTEEN

Clare is the first to arrive. The porter takes her coat and the banqueting manager shows her into the room prepared for the lunch. Portraits of Liberal statesmen of the last century, some of them copies, the originals having been sold when the club ran into financial difficulties between the wars, gaze imperturbably down on the long oval table, crisp with white linen and twinkling, under the lit chandeliers, with polished cutlery and glass. There is an arrangement of white lilies in the centre, which Clare considers funereal rather than celebratory but she decides not to interfere: it is too late to change the table decorations now. She lays her own offering, a long-stemmed, single scarlet rose, beside Silas's place, and turns her attention to the other end of the room, which has been stripped for preprandial mingling.

Clare says, to the banqueting manager,

'Don't you think it might be better if there were a few chairs about? It's a hundredth birthday, after all. My step-papa is a conscientious host. He'll never sit down if all his guests are standing. Just a few small tables with three or four chairs each would give the right kind of invitation, I think . . .' And, when he looks doubtful, 'Come on, I'll give you a hand.'

She advances towards the far end of the room where the tables and chairs that usually occupy the cleared space have been carefully stacked out of sight behind the long trestle that is serving as a bar. When Coral and Will enter the room, Clare is triumphantly manoeuvring a smallish round table between the end of the trestle and the wall of the room, pulling aside the cloth that covers the trestle and making the glasses totter and jangle, while the man in charge looks helplessly on.

'That's better,' Clare says, placing the table in the middle of the empty space. 'Now all we need are some chairs and he'll have somewhere to sit and put his glass, and other people can sit with him and have a proper chat.'

She beams at Coral and Will. 'Isn't that better? How lovely to see you. You were wonderful on the telly the other day, Coral darling. I was working, of course, we working women can't watch in the middle of the day, but I taped it. Terribly good, I thought, and you looked so amazingly *young*! Are you doing anything at the moment?' And without waiting for an answer, 'Will, you *are* better, aren't you? Your darling old dad has been so wretchedly worried.'

She comes up to Coral and Will and kisses them both firmly on the lips, an intimacy that Will finds enjoyable, Coral somewhat less so. She endures it, however, with a better grace than she might have done if she had not had news from her agent this morning that pleased her. She has been offered the part of Macbeth in an all-woman production at the Almeida, and although she doesn't, in theory, approve of this sort of gender conceit, it will be better for her reputation than playing a post-menopausal hag in a serial comedy about dinner ladies or charwomen.

She says, smiling, 'Thank you, Clare, I'm glad you enjoyed *Magistrate.* Of course I *was* a lot younger then! And I have a major part in the Scottish play in September, not much money but a very interesting production, which should get a lot of notice if not necessarily praise, and so I'll be in rehearsal during the summer. If you're free, and if it would amuse you to come to the opening night, I'll see you get sent a ticket.'

And she moves away, still politely smiling, towards her sisters-in-law, Hannah and Alice, who have just come into the room, leaving Will (so she tells herself) at Clare's mercy.

'You're looking very well, Clare,' Will says, and then, vaguely recalling something Alice had said to him recently, some stricture or other, 'I mean, very pretty indeed.'

Which she does, he thinks, a little surprised at himself for the warm access of pleasure he immediately feels. She isn't as plump as Bella. She is, of course, younger. Thirty-nine, he seems to remember. A nice age, eyes still wonderfully clear, neck still unlined, upper arms still rounded and firm.

Why should he think of Clare's upper arms? They are not, after all, on show at the moment; in fact, she is appropriately and modestly covered for this wintry weather. For the most part, that is. Under a neat, short blue jacket she is wearing a low-necked white silk shirt that drapes becomingly in the front, so that from Will's height, he can see the lace edging of her brassiere and the lovely swellings of her breasts.

He has never thought of Clare as being an attractive woman before. Perhaps she has been too young up to now. Will has never been much taken by extreme youth; having daughters, he has always thought, is likely to put any reasonable man off nymphets.

He says, suddenly jovial, 'It really is good to see you. I was only saying to Father the other day, we don't see nearly enough of you. Ridiculous, when we live in the same city. I suppose one falls into habits. And, of course,

253

having a spouse in the theatre does limit one's social life. That is, when she is acting in the legit theatre, of course, most filming and telly work takes place in the day . . .'

He hears himself running on and feels foolish. But Clare appears to be listening closely and seriously, her eyes never leaving his face. Her eyes have remarkably clear whites and long lashes. It strikes him that she is looking at him far more carefully than she could have looked at Coral or she would surely have said something like, 'What have you done to your poor eye?' Though the damage has been well disguised, Coral having worked hard on concealment this morning, it is still visible to someone with normal vision. Perhaps Clare was just being tactful.

She says now, 'It really is wonderful to see you looking so well. I must tell you, I have been praying—and I mean that, on my knees *praying*—that you would be all right for today. It means so much to him.' She smiles very fully and sweetly. 'I do love him so much, you know. I really do love your dear father.'

A bit soulful, Will thinks, though he is touched by her concern, which is so obviously genuine. There is absolutely no reason why it should make him uncomfortable. It is not as if Coral were in earshot. He says, 'Thank you,' which he realises is not quite the right response to her declaration of love for Silas. 'I mean for your prayers, of course!' he continues brightly, and sees, with a measure of relief, that Silas has just entered the room. He smiles at Clare, touching her shoulder affectionately, to show her he is sorry to leave her.

Silas is leaning on two sticks, and looking distinctly ill; hollow and grey in the face and dragging his left leg a little. All been too much for him; even for Silas an occasion like this must generate a degree of social anxiety! Will tells himself he should have spent yesterday evening dining at the club, keeping his father company, not sitting up too late and drinking too much with Coral and Alice. A wave of guilt washes over him. His concern for his father has never matched his father's concern for him. He thinks of the old man flying in at a moment's notice from wherever he happens to be to his only son's bedside, the reliably regular letters and faxes, and, further back, almost forgotten until Alice mentioned it recently, the elaborate web of lies and pretences woven around Mother's last illness . . .

'Not good for a growing boy to have a mad mother.' Is it possible that Father once said that when Will could have heard him? Or is it something Alice has told him Father had said? Or is it an extrapolation from Father's known opinions and cadences. After all these years any one of Silas's children can probably summon up what he would say, and how he would say it, in most situations.

'Ah, Will!' Silas presses his cold cheek against Will's, digging it in, bone to bone; his customary, affectionate greeting.

Will says, 'Happy returns.'

Silas grunts. 'I sincerely hope not.'

'Happy birthday, then.'

'I very much doubt it. You enjoy it, though. I told them to bring out the wine only as it is needed. Not to be ostentatious, you know. Ah. Albert, isn't it? Albert. You remember my son?'

Will shakes hands with a man of much his own age who he supposes must be the son of his father's banker, or maybe his lawyer or doctor; the son, anyway, of someone who was once of consequence to Silas. This man says, gravely, 'I think we have never met. Albert Kastner, from Switzerland. My grandfather took care of your father's affairs, then my father. I now do my best to carry on the tradition. Your father is an exceptional man. This is a great occasion.'

'It's good of you to come.'

'It is my pleasure.'

Albert Kastner inclines his head and turns away to accept a glass of champagne from a waiter. He has seen Will as part of the receiving line, not someone with whom he needs to make conversation. Feeling rebuked, even if unintentionally, Will turns back to Silas but his father is surrounded now, busily talking, managing perfectly well on his own.

Apart from the family and the occasional club committee members, most of Silas's other guests are known to Will, if not by sight, by guesswork. That man is Father's banker's son, that one, his dentist—from the same family that has kept his genetically excellent teeth in his head all these years. (Will was taken to see this man's great-uncle when he was seven or so, an occasion he remembers as terrifying, though he no longer knows if this was due to his own frailty and cowardice or something that actually happened on that occasion.)

Will also recognises, though distantly, the elderly man Silas is now putting through his bony-cheek routine—a painful experience only imposed upon the especially favoured. A Dutchman—no, a Dane. Jensen? Jansen? The son of a man Silas had known in the war. Will is interested to see a rare tear running down his father's face. He is about to join him and Jensen—Otto Jensen, he recalls now, from a lunch at the club a good many years ago now, before Bella—but Silas is keeping Otto with him as he trawls the room, displaying his excellent memory for faces and names as he makes introductions. He has given his left stick to Otto, and is using him as a crutch; either because another man gives him better support than the stick, or because he wants to keep this guest close beside him.

Will is wondering—too late, of course—if he should have offered his arm to his father,

257

when his sister, Hannah, throws her arms around him, kissing him smackingly first on one cheek, then on another. Her perfume is light and flowery, but she has made too heavy a use of it. Will says, 'You managed to get here, Hannah dear! Good for you! I like your dress. What a pretty blue!'

'Julius wanted me to get something new but I thought, What's the point, no one's going to look at me, old women are always invisible, and Julius has always said that blue suits me. How *are* you, Will darling? What do you think about Coral playing Macbeth? She's just told me. Mind you, she's got the height for it and of course he's not one of Shakespeare's masculine men, but between you and me and the proverbial gatepost I think it's a pretty silly idea. Still, as Julius says, the whole point of the theatre is artifice, no one is playing himself, or herself in this case, so why ever not? I only wish I could come down to see her but I don't think I could manage to sit through an evening at the theatre, too claustrophobic for me, though the Almeida is very fashionable now, isn't it? Not that that makes any difference, of course.'

More for the sake of saying something than because he has anything to say, Will speaks. 'It's not a very good theatre for the vertiginous. It used to be a medical lecture theatre, I think, rows of students looking down at the Professor dissecting a body on stage.

Hannah—we ought to move around, don't you think? Some of these people may not know anyone.'

'They all look cheerful enough to me. Lots of drink, food to come, why shouldn't they be? Oh, all right, as long as I don't have to be agreeable to you-know-who, I'll do my best. I haven't looked at the placement. Who am I next to?'

'Mrs Newhouse, I don't know her but she's Martin Mudd's daughter. An address in the country, sounds like a farm so I thought you might have something in common. You've got Julius opposite. I thought that would be comfortable for you. And you are on the side of the table near to the door.'

Hannah beams at him. Will finds that he feels both sorry for and fond of this large, sad, older sister. He says, 'Do you think Father might like to sit down at that little table till lunch is ready? Why don't you go and suggest it? I'm sure he'd like you to join him.'

He watches Hannah make her stately way towards Silas who appears to accept her suggestion. Otto Jensen on one side and Hannah on the other, he limps to the table and sinks into a chair beside it with an air of relief. Arriving at Will's side, Alice mutters, 'He looks a bit peaky, don't you think? Well, more than that, I wonder if we ought to get Davey to look at him.'

'Now? I should think he'd be furious.'

'He likes Davey. Always ringing him up and asking his advice on this or that. Gets it free that way.'

'All the same.'

'I suppose you're right,' Alice concedes. Then, with a grin, 'He's very dishy, is Davey. We've just been talking. Or rather, I have, and he listens as if I'm the Delphic Oracle. Or had just won the Nobel. One of the doctors in his practice heard me speak in Cambridge the other day, and Davey says she hasn't stopped telling him how inspiring I was. Very good for the ego, and our Davey passes on this kind flattery so very nicely, worshipful, you know, but sizing me up at the same time, almost to the point of asking me if I'm up for it. Very sexy, that sort of approach. Besides, he looks as if he washes every day which could be an improvement on Jake.'

Will says, 'Don't you dare, Alice.'

'No? Oh, well, if you feel strongly about it!'

'You're sitting next to his wife. She teaches zoology. So I expect you'll get plenty of adulation during lunch if that's what you want. And you've got Otto Jensen, too. He's a physicist. Intellectual stimulus on both sides and no hanky-panky.'

Alice says, thoughtfully, 'Jensen, well, his father, I suppose, was the man who brought the Jewish girl to England. The one who stayed with Aunt Geneva. I'll remember her name in a minute.'

But Will is looking at his watch. 'Time we sat down, I think. Keep an eye on Father, will you, Alice? I'll go and alert the head waiter.'

* * *

The first course, smoked eel, is already on the table. Silas says, loudly, 'I thought I ordered soup.'

Coral, passing behind him, bends and shouts in his ear. 'You changed your mind, Daddy. You told me two days ago about the smoked eel, remember? We had a long talk on the phone.'

Silas twists awkwardly round to look up at her. 'If you say so. What have you done to your eye?' He gives her one of his wicked, whiskery grins. 'Don't tell me the boy has turned into a wife-beater.'

'Walked into a door handle, Daddy,' Coral says, teasing him. 'I believe that's the conventional excuse, isn't it? A proper gent will accept it, so you mind your manners now.'

'Never known a handle fixed high enough on a door to poke a tall girl like you in the eye.' Silas is hanging on to Coral's hand; a lifeline, perhaps? Like Will, Coral wonders if this is all turning out too overwhelming for the poor man. His fault, on the other hand. He had insisted on inviting what Coral thinks of as *extras*. All these peripheral people, sons and daughters of the main characters, long since

261

dead.

She says, 'I'd better go and sit down, Daddy Not far away. On your side of the table, opposite Will, so I can record his speech. You'll be all right between these two lovely ladies.'

She smirks at Clare, and smiles at the club chairman's wife on Silas's other side, who looks a nice woman, calm as well as pretty.

Silas says, 'Remind Will. I don't want any nonsense about reading out telegrams. Worshipful Company of Ironmongers, that sort of thing. Not an ironmonger among them nowadays, shouldn't wonder. No one wants to listen to that sort of rubbish. I had a lot of cards this morning with damn silly jokes on them, well, you know where they went! Straight into the bin.'

He is still holding fast to Coral's hand. She raises her eyebrow at Clare, who comes to her rescue. She says, in a high, clear voice, smooth and sweet as ice cream, 'Popsicle, darling, you haven't said hallo to me properly And you haven't once looked at your beautiful present.'

She picks up the scarlet rose and waves it in front of his nose—to Coral's mind, *wiggles* is the word for this feebly flirtatious gesture—and Silas, startled, releases Coral's hand.

Silas says, 'I was wondering where it came from. Thought it might have been left over from last night's banquet decorations. Very pretty, Clare, my dear. Thank you.'

262

Clare purrs, 'What else do you give the man who has everything, except one perfect rose?'

Coral pats her father-in-law on the shoulder, silently commiserating with him, although she knows he neither needs nor wants sympathy. Only too delighted, the silly old fool, to have that moist-eyed harlot smooching over him!

Suddenly, as she makes her way to her seat, Coral finds herself in indignantly righteous accord with Hannah. *That girl*—she still looks like a girl, ripe and rosy as a plum—might easily be totally venal, out for all she could get. No normal human being talks and behaves in that soppy and sentimental way *naturally*. Unless they are dim-witted, or drunk. Clare's an educated woman, for God's sake, a lawyer! Coral moves her lips silently as she speaks to herself. Watching her suck up to the old man like that, does make you wonder about her mother . . .

By the time Coral reaches her seat, she is grinning broadly. Before she sits down, she looks hard at her husband, absorbedly chatting to the youngish woman next to him.

Her innocent husband, Will, who would never have a word said against Bella . . .

Then she sits down herself, next to Bella's son and Clare's brother. Davey.

*   *   *

Roast pheasant follows the smoked eel, and after the pheasant, a sorbet. Then two whole, large Stilton cheeses are put on the table at the same time as bowls of the pudding: peeled green grapes covered with whipped double cream and a scattering of soft brown sugar on top of the cream, which has been under the grill just long enough for the sugar to melt and get crusty. This pudding, Silas knows, is not to everyone's taste, hence the Stilton, but he has developed a sweet tooth in his old age and this is his favourite. A double helping this lunchtime is his birthday present to himself.

When the coffee is brought round and the club chairman gets up to speak, Silas checks his pudding plate to make sure he has still got enough to occupy him during the speeches, which he will not be able to hear. He nods at the chairman, who is looking in his direction and so, presumably, saying something agreeable about him, thanking him for the lunch, perhaps, some flattery about *our oldest member*, but he might be making a political harangue in Chinese for all Silas can understand and although he does try to maintain an intelligent and listening expression, it becomes too much of an effort and his thoughts drift away . . .

*   *   *

Coral sees his attention fade. She doubts if

264

other people will notice it; that infinitesimal slackening of the muscles round the eyes and the mouth. Poor old boy, the chairman won't go on for long but then he has his son's speech to contend with and Will is bound to look at him from time to time to see how he's taking it. Coral rehearsed Will for the third time this morning and persuaded him to cut it down to twelve minutes which, being more used to the written than the spoken word, he seemed to find difficult. She is resigned to the knowledge that, once he is on his feet and beyond her control, he will reinstate the passages she deleted. There is an hour on the tape, anyway; she has thought she might, afterwards, get a few of his old mates—his old mates' children and grandchildren—to ad-lib into the small microphone, tell the odd tale to amuse him. She might even take a leaf out of that tiresome young woman's book and tell the old devil how much she admires his courage in battling on.

The chairman has finished. A nice, graceful speech, what an honour for the club, etc., etc. Will is shuffling his few pages and looking anxious. He is not a natural speechmaker. And the tiresome young woman is repeating the gist of the chairman's piece into Silas's ear, one pretty paw softly cupping his chin. She has a sweet voice but turned up to full volume it is, for those of normal hearing, quite distressingly shrill.

And Coral, who has had enough wine to put

her comfortably in what she thinks of as the freedom zone—that is, free to speak her mind clearly, without mumbling, or in any way incurring an accusation of drunkenness—leans towards Will and says softly, 'Our Little Screamer!'

And realises, too late, that she has Davey beside her. She turns to him to make what amends she can, and finds him spluttering with near-silent laughter.

*   *   *

Will is on his feet now. Silas presumes he has begun with a joke. Everyone within Silas's vision is laughing. And very silly they look too: mouths open, teeth smeared with the food they have eaten, faces darkened with too much expensive burgundy. Would have been more sensible to turn on the club claret but that banqueting manager had rather turned up his nose when he suggested it. He should have stuck to his guns. Well, he did over the champagne. Sainsbury's was quite good enough, they certainly drank a lot of it, he didn't exactly see anyone tipping it into a potted plant, or whatever people do nowadays when the wine is disgusting.

He wonders how long the boy will go on. He has almost finished his grapes-in-cream pudding. It was Gladys Ogilvie who introduced it to him, about the only good thing she ever did for him. Though it was more likely her cook who had invented it. When they were first married, Effie showed him the notebook of recipes the Ogilvie cook had printed out for her, big black capitals, full of warnings. BEEF OVERCOOKED IS RUINED. That sort of thing. Effie had never cooked anything before in her life. The grape pudding was the first dish she made for him, carrying it into the dining room, her face flushed, earnestly watching his as he took his first mouthful. Such a pretty little thing, graceful, breakable . . .

Pity.

She made grapes-in-cream for Aunt's birthday one year. When was that? He had the old Invicta then. Hannah was a baby in a basket on the back seat and Effie sat beside him in the front, holding the dish out in front of her, scolding if he braked suddenly, or took a corner too fast. She had the bag of soft brown sugar between her feet. The sugar was to be sprinkled over the top at the last minute, just before it went under the grill. He can't remember now whether Aunt enjoyed the pudding or not. She probably said something like, 'You shouldn't have gone to all that trouble, you know.'

Thinking of Aunt, and the grapes-in-cream, and that uncomfortable journey from Norwich, he grins broadly. Then realises that no one at the table is smiling. The boy is making a serious point, nothing to laugh at. Luckily, they are all watching him, not looking at Silas. As far as Silas can see, anyway.

No more private jokes. Better to keep a stone face, only smile when the others smile.

He will have to reply. Difficult, in the circumstances. Best to come right out with it, say he can't reply to the boy's speech since he couldn't hear what he said, although thanks to his good daughter-in-law he will be able to listen later on at his leisure. Have to say something about Will in return. How he was there at his birth. Should he say something about his mother being long past the age when she should have had children? Effie had only been forty. Women have babies when they are well over forty nowadays, and they wouldn't thank you for calling them elderly mothers. Not only that, husbands have to be there all the time, through the whole gory business, disgusting in his view.

Better leave that. Obstetrics isn't his field. Of course, he could set them all by the ears, cat among the pigeons if he had a mind to make mischief. *Will doesn't know it, his sisters don't know it, not a living soul knows it, but I'm not his father. Will is the son of a man who used to call himself Dolly.* And/or *The tale we've always stuck to is that his poor mother went out of her mind but the truth is she drank herself to death and no one could stop her.*

Better not. Hardly fair when Effie is not here to put her side of either matter. And even if being a bastard is not a disgrace any longer, it might upset the boy who, apart from young Clare, is the only living person who strikes much of a chord in him. Though if the dear little puss thinks she is going to put her pretty paws on any more of his money she is sadly mistaken.

Aunt would say, 'You've done well by him.' And Bella? 'What else could you do? Throw them both out in the winter snow?'

What is he going to say to these people? 'Speaking as the only centenarian among you I can tell you that no one, in my view, should be allowed to linger so long'?

He will have to mention his daughters. He can't say too much about Alice and her achievements without making it seem he is disappointed in his other daughter. The only way he could make it clear that he thought Hannah had done equally well with her life would be to come straight out with it and say that to his mind the proper place for a married woman is at home looking after her family. Not a popular opinion nowadays. Nor an argument he cares to get into.

'No point in fighting useless battles unless you care with your whole heart and soul.' Who said that? Or something like it. Molly. When? Wait a minute, it's coming . . . When she was trying to persuade Aunt to let her go to London, to the Royal Academy of Dramatic Art. Aunt had said something about her 'useless'—or perhaps it was 'foolish' or 'hopeless'—fight to become an actress. She would only fail, she said, better to go into the Post Office where she would be sure of success. And Molly, standing in the door of the scullery, the sunlight behind her making a glorious halo out of her hair, had fought for her dream, for her future . . .

Oh, Molly Molly. Why aren't you here? And Aunt. And Hans. And Effie and Bella—though that might cause problems. Nothing new in that, on the other hand, both his wives have made trouble for him. Even Bella, who did make him happy, cheated him over the money, dying before him . . .

* * *

Will is sitting down now. He smiles at his father. And Silas, whose world is peopled with the dead, stands up slowly and painfully, to speak to the living.